Love Chronicles

 E. L. Dailey

RoseDog Books

PITTSBURGH, PENNSYLVANIA 15238

RoseDog Books
585 Alpha Drive
Pittsburgh, PA 15238
Visit our website at *www.rosedogbookstore.com*

ISBN: 978-1-4809-7215-5
eISBN 978-1-4809-7192-9

 Table of Contents

How to Mend a Broken Heart

On a stormy, fall day in the city of Washington D.C. In a courtroom, there she sits next to her lawyer, as the judge carries out his decision on a bitter divorce for twenty-nine-year-old Angela Jones. Angela is a soft-spoken, beautiful, caramel complexioned, woman. Though the judge has rewarded heavily in her favor, she has the look on her face as if she has lost it all. This is not the life Angela dreamed of at all. The only thing she ever wanted was to be happy with her husband of six years. Though it did not work in her favor, Angela remains a calm presence in the midst of her divorce.

On this same stormy afternoon, in an apartment not too far from the courthouse, lived Angela's cousin Melissa. Melissa is a full figured, beautiful, black woman. Though they are the same age, Melissa has always been like a big sister to Angela. Melissa is the youngest of three children (two brothers). Angela grew up as an only child. They were always inseparable. The two even chose to go into the medical field together. As Angela's case was in session, Melissa baby sat Angela's five-year old son Chris. Melissa, an independent woman, has been looking for a roommate to split the rent. Little did she know that her luck was about to change when she received a knock at the door.

"Who is it?" she answers.

"I'm here about the roommate ad" Melissa opens the door and sees this masculine, handsome man.

"Hi, my name is Malik Jackson. I'm here about the roommate ad." Melissa stares for a brief second as if she's tearing away his clothes with her eyes.

"Oh, well, come on in." Melissa says. Malik comes in, sits down with Melissa, and begin discussing business. As they come to an agreement, little Chris enters the room.

"Is this your son?" he asks.

"No, this is my little cousin, Chris. I'm his babysitter." Melissa says.

After further discussion Malik then adds that once his background check is cleared he'll move in.

On a Saturday night, it has been two days since Angela's big day in court. Melissa, always looking out for Angela's best interest, took her out to the club to ease her mind. Angela, still hurt from her bitter divorce, was turning down every man whom approached her. Melissa, however, was enjoying the night, as she sat next to Angela with a drink and said, "Angie, you need to be getting your drink on. I brought you here to have a goodtime, and you won't even dance." "I'm good." Angela says. Melissa, with such concern says to Angela, "Girl, everything's gonna be alright." As the music plays Melissa sees Malik and invites him to their table. Melissa introduces Malik to Angela. Malik can't help but notice how pretty Angela is. Sitting there, long curly hair pinned up with those beautiful green eyes. A hot song starts to play. Melissa then goes back to the dance floor, leaving Angela alone with Malik. Angela and Malik each were feeling awkward as he proceeds to break the ice.

"So Angela, you dance much?" he asks as she shakes her head. "Well, would you care to dance with me?" he asks.

"No, thanks I don't really feel like it." she says.

"May I at least buy you a drink?" Angela, so wrapped up in hurt and frustration snaps angrily at Malik.

"Look, Malcolm or whatever your name is. I really don't feel like talking are anything right now, and I'd appreciate you not pushing up on me OK!" Malik, with a stunned look on his face, is completely blown away. In a word he was speechless as he refused to return fire.

"Okay then, you have a nice night." he says as he gets up and leave. After the song goes off, Melissa comes back to the table and finds Angela alone.

"Where's Malik?" she asks.

"Who cares." Angela says with a nonchalant look. Melissa, then realizing Angela must have said something cruel.

"Angie, what did you say to him? You can't take out your anger on every man now. I'm not gonna watch you do the diary of a mad black woman thing." Melissa, then says, "So what you and I are about to do before we leave, is have that drink I brought you here for with your mad ass." Melissa gets up and in a joking manner says, "The man ain't even moved into my apartment yet, and you ready to run him off. Come on let's go by the bar. Getting me all worked up for nothing. Is my wig on straight?" Angela walks alongside Melissa to bar, finally cracking a smile and snickering. This is so like them. Whenever Angela was down, she could always count on Melissa to be there for her. Like a big sister.

A few weeks later Malik moved in and is now Melissa's new roommate. After a hard day's work on the construction site, Malik comes home. He showers then eats a home cooked meal provided by Melissa. After dinner they sit out on the patio of their upstairs apartment, as they get to know each other.

"So what brings you from Tennessee all the way up here to Chocolate City?" she asks.

"I was at a crossroad in my life and I just needed a change for a moment." Malik says.

"I hear you."

"So where's your little cousin?" Malik asks.

"Chris? He's with his mom thank goodness. She didn't have class tonight, so he's with her. You remember my cousin Angela, from the other night at the club?"

"Oh yeah, the Ice Woman" he recalls.

"Angie's okay, she's just going through a lot right now with her divorce and all." she says.

"Oh, well, I can relate to that." he says.

"Really…Are you divorced?"

Yeah for about three months now." he explains as they talk and get more acquainted with each other.

As weeks go by Chris is around on evenings when Angela attends school getting her Doctor's degree. Malik, already a father of two, develops a bond with Chris. As a result in this, Melissa whom is always concerned about Angela now gets an idea to play match maker. Melissa looks out of the curtain from their apartment; she sees Malik on the playground putting in time with Chris and gets an idea of putting Angela and Malik together.

It is a busy day at the Infirmary, where Melissa and Angela work. During the day whenever Angela and Melissa talk, Melissa tends to bring up Malik's name. When they sit down in the lunchroom to eat, Melissa starts up again.

"Malik sure is great with Chris. They stay out on the playground together, and he's always buying him some new toy." Angela eats her lunch as she looks at Melissa in an unimpressed manner.

"Melissa, you've been carrying on about him all day long."

"I'm just saying, ever since your little run in with him when you two met, you haven't said anything to him. He's really a nice guy Angie."

"Well, if he's that much of a good person then why don't you date him?" Angela says.

"Girl, you know I'm still with Andre. All I'm saying is get to know him. It's not like I'm trying to hook you up or anything." Melissa, trying desperately to put on her best innocent face, but Angela knows her all too well.

"Sure you're not." Angela says.

See every time Angela has a bad breakup, Melissa tends to set her up with a friend. Not to interfere, she just hates to see Angela down. So Melissa invites Angela to come over Friday for dinner.

Friday arrives and Malik is off for the weekend. He has to stop at the supermarket for a few items for the dinner Melissa has planned. As he comes back out of the store he sees this fine, long legged Puerto Rican girl in a nice fitted skirt and stilettoes named Nichelle Perez whom seems to be having car trouble. Through their conversation, he finds that she's from the same apartment complex as he. So he introduces himself and asks if she needs a hand. He then takes a look at her car.

"Looks like it's the battery." he says. She explains that she just got off work, and is going to be late for her part-time job. Malik, being the guy he is, offers to jumpstart her car so she can get home. He also offers to drop her off at work.

In spite of having dinner with that snobby ass Angela

So where's your part-time job?" Malik asks.

"Peepers" Nichelle says as Malik curiously looks at her.

"Isn't that a, um"

"A gentlemen's club" she cuts him off. "I just do it for the excitement. Besides I'm single with no kids." Nichelle explains. Malik makes it back to the apartment where he tells Melissa that something came up and he can't stay. Melissa is now furious with Malik.

"What do you mean something came up? Malik, how you gonna do this? Angie is going to be here any minute now."

Come on Melissa, your cousin's got issues. She's got her ass on her shoulders and she doesn't even speak to me when she comes to pick up Chris."

As the two go back and forth, the doorbell rings. It's Angela, Chris, and Angela's mother. They come in, and Melissa is about to introduce them, when suddenly, Chris goes over to Malik, and Malik picks him up.

"Will you look at that? Boy, he don't want to hold your bad self. Get down." says Angela's mom.

"He's alright, this is my little friend right here." says Malik as Angela looks.

"Everybody, this is my roommate, Malik. Malik, this is my Aunt Synitha, and you already know Angie." Melissa says.

As they come on in and talk, the doorbell rings again. Angela goes back and opens the door. It's Nichelle, from next door, now wearing a black leather cat suit.

"Hi, I'm looking for Malik." she says.

Now how ironic is this? Angela can't help but think about all the good things Melissa had to say about Malik. Now there is some floozy at the door for him.

"Yeah, come on in. Malik, someone's here to see you." Angela smiles in a disappointed like manner. Everyone is now looking at this awkward situation. Malik, feels somewhat embarrassed, not of Nichelle, but of what they must think of him. Malik introduces Nichelle and is about to leave, when Melissa calls him into the kitchen. Melissa explains to Malik that the dinner is actually for Angela's birthday. Malik now feels remorse for not staying as he leaves with Nichelle.

A few days has passed since Angela's birthday, and three days until Thanksgiving. Melissa is babysitting again, but has to run an errand. Angela arrives by to pick up Chris. Malik was babysitting him as he slept and in the middle of watching football. Angel rings the doorbell as Malik comes to the door to let her in. He opens the door as Angela notices but tries desperately not to look at how his muscles bulge through the tank top he wore as she comes in.

"Hey, Melissa went to the beauty store, but she needs to see you before you leave." he says. Angela takes a seat next to him and her sleeping son. In an attempt to make up for spoiling her birthday, Malik gives her a gift. "Angela it seems as if we keep getting off to a bad start. I had no idea that it was your birthday. So, I went and got you a little something. I hope you like it." he says. He gives her a gift bag. She pulls out a porcelain figurine of a little girl in doctor's attire.

"Thank you. It's beautiful." she says. Angela absolutely loves it and is now thinking that maybe he's not so bad.

"So who's playing?" she asks about the game.

Washington and Tennessee" he says.

"Oh yeah, I forgot we had to play tonight."

"What do you mean **we**, you watch football?"

"Are you kidding? I grew up a Washington fan." she says. So for the next twenty minutes or so, they cheer for opposite teams, argue calls, and laugh.

Angela and Malik get more acquainted as Melissa comes home and asks Angela to do her nails for her date with Andre. As Angela does Melissa's nails, they talk about their planned trip to visit their Grandmother in South Carolina. Angela tells Melissa that she's not going, but her mother and Chris still are. Angela, being newly divorced, really does not feel much like celebrating Thanksgiving.

While Angela and Melissa continue to talk, Malik gets a call on his cell phone. It's his mother along with his little girls. Angela eavesdrops on Malik's conversation. She learns that he won't be able to make it home for Thanksgiving due to car trouble. Just hearing Malik playing with his children over the phone, and knowing how good he is to Chris, Angela starts to feel sympathy for him. That night when she put Chris to bed she immediately began to think about Malik once more.

The following Tuesday morning Angela went to the airport to drop off her mother and son. Malik was also there to drop off Melissa. They say their goodbyes and board their plane. Malik and Angela talk on their way out to the parking lot.

"So are you just going to spend Thanksgiving alone Angie?" he asks.

"Yeah, I just need some time to myself that's all." she replies.

"Oh, I can understand that. Sometimes you just need some me time, huh." he says. Angela then turns toward Malik, already knowing his situation.

"So, what about you?" she asks.

"I don't have much of a choice." he says.

"Well, what if you did? I mean, if you want I could take you to be with your family." Malik tries to be modest but ends up accepting Angela's offer.

the crack of dawn next morning, Malik and Angela set out on a thirteen-hour drive to Tennessee. As they were riding the Isley Brother's song 'Groove with you' came on the radio.

"Oh turn that up." Angela says.

"What you know about this?"

"I know all about the Isley Brothers thank you." Angela smirks as they begin to see each other in a different light. Along the way they get more and more acquainted with each other as they talk, laugh and sight-see. At one of their stops, Angela and Malik took a selfie together with each other's phone. During their trip, at one point, Malik looked over at her as she slept peacefully in spite of all the heartache she'd been through.

they got closer to their destination, Malik called his mother to surprise her of his arrival. To his surprise, his uncle, aunt, and a host of cousins were in town, staying at his mother's. As a result, they went to rent a room. They come upon the last motel in town with only one vacancy for a single room in which they got the room and unpacked.

"Would you like to go get something to eat?" Malik asks Angela.

"Sure."

Malik took Angela to Danny's dine, drink and dance, (or as the locals call it the 4 D's). At the 4 D's you can dine in the front section, but in the back you can enjoy the club scene. Malik talked Angela into trying some of their famous hot wings.

"Malik these are good." she says.

"I thought you'd like them." Malik says.

While enjoying their wings, Malik's best friend Ray comes by speaks before heading into the club. Malik asks Angela if she'd like to go inside.

"Sure." she says.

They go into the club section where Ray was. Malik and Ray talk for a minute, Ray then asks Angela to dance. Angela smiles as if she's going to say no, but Malik talks her into having some fun.

Oh, you gonna dance tonight Angie. We're not going to leave until you do." he says. She laughs and goes on the dance floor with Ray. They dance as Ray's wife Tameka comes in. She immediately spots Malik and starts to talk with him as he then introduces her to his friend Angela. Angela comes out of her shell little by little as Malik and Ray take turns buying rounds and telling old stories. Angela was unaware that she kept standing closer to Malik as the night went on. At this point Malik is starting to develop feelings towards her. All four decide to go onto the dance floor. As they dance Malik and Ray show off some moves.

The DJ then plays Keith Sweat's 'Right and wrong way'. Angela and Malik look at each other. Angela was about to leave the dance floor. Malik then gently took her by the hand and held her very close. For the next few minutes Angela and Malik were miles away from reality, lost in each other's eyes, as the music played.

Malik was constantly reminded of how beautiful Angela was as he stared into her luscious green eyes. Angela was mesmerized by the way Malik held her in his arms. The scent of his cologne had drawn her in like a type of pheromone. She felt him thrusting against her. The song came to a close as Angela and Malik's eyes were dead locked. They were face to face and out of nowhere Angela lunged forward and kissed Malik. In an instant she realized where she was.

"Oh, I'm, I'm sorry." Angela says.

"I hear you boy, get that sugar!" Ray says all loud and country like.

"Leave them alone!" Tameka says. Angela was so embarrassed that she headed straight to the ladies room. She looked in the mirror, trying to get a grip on what had just happened. Angela was soon joined by Tameka.

So you and Malik are pretty serious huh. How long y'all been together?" Angela was unsure on how to respond. She attempts, but no words come out. "You know what, it don't even matter girl. I'm just glad to see the old Malik back. When Ray and I had problems Malik was always there for us. When Nesha left him he just wasn't the same, but he finally divorced her and moved on. He's a good person and everything so take care of him."

"I will." Angela says.

Angela returns from the restroom with Tameka, she notices Malik was looking all serious and Ray was talking loud and swearing about something.

"Dude looks like he got an eye problem over there!" Ray says angrily.

"Well, looks like our fun is over with. Girl get Malik and let's go." Tameka says as Angela tries to convince Malik to leave.

"Come on Malik, let's go." Angela says as Malik stood there with a mean look. Angela then stood in front of him.

"Malik, please, let's go." she says as they all left then club.

At the motel they prepare for bed. Angela asked Malik about the guy at the club. Malik told Angela that the guy was an old friend that he fell out with.

"I'm sorry about the way I acted in the club."

"Do you mean the kiss?" Malik asked.

"No, I mean the way I treated you the night we first met. You didn't deserve that Malik." she explains. Angela then opens up about how her husband just up and left her and Chris. Angela sits at the edge of the bed as tears start to stream from her eyes as she talks about all the heartache and pain he caused her. Malik sits next to her with comforting words.

Sometimes bad things happen to good people. Look Angie, I'm not gonna give you that God has a plan speech, but I really do believe that things happen for a reason. You are a very beautiful, intelligent woman with a lot going for yourself. A lot of guys I know would love to have someone like you, I know I would. You're a tough mom too, I see how you chastise Chris when he acts up." She smiles and wipes her eyes. Malik puts his arm around Angela.

"You're going to be alright Angie." he says to her. "And you're not spending Thanksgiving alone. You're coming with me tomorrow and I'm not taking no for an answer." he says.

It is now Thanksgiving Day as the aroma of turkey, ham, sweet potato pie, and cakes fill the air. The women are gossiping and cooking. The children are outside playing. The men are cheering as the game is on. Malik and Angela arrive and are at the door.

"Now Angela, no matter how many times we tell them we're just friends, they are still going to call you my girlfriend. So just go along with it." Angela looks at him with a smirk.

"Malik!" she then sighs. "Alright, but you owe me big time."

Malik and Angela go inside and are greeted by his family as he introduces her. She then meets his daughters Malisha and Jasmine.

"Aw! Malik, they are so precious." she says. Angela goes into the room and sits next to Malik. His mother says to her, "Come on child let them ole men folk watch their game."

As the day goes on they eat Thanksgiving dinner, talk and laugh. Angela feels right at home with Malik's family. She watches Malik put in time with his daughters until their mother comes to pick them up.

The day comes to a close as the temperature drops drastically. Malik says goodbye to his family as he and Angela prepare to leave. "Well, Ms. Angela, you come on back and see us again sometime." Malik's mother says to Angela. "Yes ma'am, I will."

On their way back to the motel Malik pulls into the driveway of an unlit home. He explains to Angela that it was the house he was building before his divorce. "Would you like to see it?" he asked just before they go in. Malik turns on the lights and shows her around. After they conclude their tour of the unfinished four bedroom brick home, they come back to the front room.

"Malik this is nice. And you're actually building this house yourself?"

"My dad and I did everything you see here. Sometimes Ray and my brother Sean come by to help. I'll move back home once it's complete."

"I started on it right after Jasmine was born." He pauses. "Not only did I find out Nesha was having an affair with my friend Dennis. It turns out that Dennis is Jasmine's biological father. So we separated for a year then just recently divorced." Angela looks at Malik with a loss for words. She stands next to Malik and holds his hand and lays her head on his shoulder.

"Just look at us, we are like two tortured souls in the dark, trying to find the light." Angela says.

On this same cold Thanksgiving night, back at the motel, Angela and Malik prepare for bed. Angela gets off the phone with Melissa. They lay in bed facing away from each other.

"I really had a great time today Malik, thank you. Your parents are nice and your cousin Frank and Uncle Mac are so crazy." she laughs.

"Yeah, they're two of a kind. I really enjoyed your company as well Angie, so thank you." Malik says. As they lie in bed, each one thinking heavily about the other. They try desperately not to though they can't help it, when their every thought is being driven by the sounds of the couple making out in the room next door getting louder and louder. Angela scoots closer to Malik.

"I'm sorry, but I can't seem to get warm enough. They need to work on this heat." Angela says.

Malik then puts his arm around her, as they now lay facing each other. Her forehead snuggled against his Adams apple. Malik rests his hand behind her neck, at the top of her back. As the couple next door gets more intense, neither Malik nor Angela can deny their lustful feelings towards each other any longer. The fact that she smelled like a flower wasn't helping either.

Angela begins to gently rub Malik's chest, as he runs his fingers through her curly hair and softly kiss her on the forehead. Angela was completely turned on as she squirms and squeezes her thighs together. Butterflies went off in her stomach as she longed to feel Malik inside of her. She felt Malik throbbing against her. He then began to kiss her in a way that would make Casanova himself blush. Malik runs his hand down Angela's back and then up her gown, grabbing the back of her lace panties, peeling them off of her. Angela lies on her back as Malik removes his underwear and gets between her legs. Malik starts kissing and sucking on Angela's neck until she can no longer stand the foreplay. She reaches down and grabs more than a handful of Malik's manhood and slides it inside of her. "Aw!" she moans in a painful, pleasant way. As they grind each other she holds his waist. "Oh Malik!" Angela screams as she climaxes. She places her hands on each side of Malik's face, kissing him heavily as he continues to penetrate inside of her. She starts to come around a second time. Malik continuously pounds deeper and deeper into Angela. She digs into Malik's back with her fingernails, about to burst again. "Oh yes! Oh yes!" She screams as Malik grimaces and lets out a groan as he comes with her. Afterwards they lay in each other arms breathless.

"This is crazy. This whole time we've been denying that we are together, now look at us." Malik says.

I know right. It's your fault." Angela teases.

"What now, do we continue to be friends and pretend that this never happened?" Malik asks.

"Malik, I really do like you, it's just that I'm scared. I don't want to be hurt again." Angela says.

"To be honest Angie, I couldn't hurt anybody right now if I tried. I especially wouldn't hurt you."

"Promise me." Angela demands.

"I promise." Malik says. And for the rest of this frigid night, Angela and Malik just lay in each other's arms.

It is now Monday, Angela and Melissa are back at work. As they are having lunch Melissa tells Angela about her seeing their grandmother and the family.

"So how was Tennessee?" Melissa asked.

"Nice, nice, it was...it was nice." Angela says with a look as if she were hiding something. Melissa looks at Angela. "What? Why are you looking at me like that?" Angela asked.

"Are you glowing?" Melissa says to Angela.

"Girl no" Angela continues to play innocent.

"You slept with Malik!" Melissa says. Angela's eyes got big as she looks around, sits her elbows on the table, and covers her face with her hand on her forehead, and smiles. "And I'll bet he was with you when you were in a hurry to get off the phone the other night...Nasty little skank." Melissa teases her.

"Okay, okay. Yes, Malik and I are seeing each other now." Angela laughs. With a huge smile, Angela then tells Melissa about her trip to Tennessee with Malik and his family.

Angela and Malik begin to spend time together at the apartment, Angela's house, the park, church, and just dinning out.

They were now in love, and are every bit of what has been missing in each other's lives.

It has been a month into their relationship. On Christmas Eve Malik was back in Tennessee with his family. Angela was in D.C. They exchanged gifts and decided to open them together over the phone. On this late night Christmas Eve, when all little children are sleeping awaiting Santa Clause. Malik calls Angela and they talk for a while. She insists that he open his gift first. Malik opens his gift which was a nice gold necklace.

"Do you like it?" she asks.

"I love it. Thanks Angie. Okay, it's your turn." Malik says. Angela opens her gift. It is a box consisting of a Teddy Bear holding a smaller box. In the small box is a diamond ring.

"Oh my God, Malik it is so beautiful. Thank you, thank you, I love it." Angela says.

"You deserve it Angie." he smiles. Angela, now so full of emotion, feels as if she could burst.

"You know when Derrick left me and Chris, I remember being so angry at life and men. I remember thinking to myself I am never going give my heart away again, and then I met you. I could not have asked for a better person to come into my life. I love you so much Malik Jackson."

I love you too Angela. Merry Christmas baby"

As the seasons progressed the love between Angela and Malik flourished. In the summer Angela earned her Doctor's degree. On the night after her graduation, Angela and Malik enjoy some alone time. She and Malik took a swim in her indoor pool. They swam then Angela sat on the edge of the pool, with her feet in the water as if she were troubled. Malik swam over and stood between her thighs and puts his arms around her waist.

"What's wrong Angie?"

"Nothing, I was just thinking what it would be like having you here with Me." Angela says to him.

"Come on Angie, we've been over this before." Malik says wearily being that they've discussed this numerous times before.

"Malik, you haven't spent one night here with me. What is it? What am I not doing?"

"It's not you Angie, I just don't want to get something started and become some live-in boyfriend, and I'm not sure if either of us are ready to take that next step again right now, you know what I mean." She nods her head.

"Yeah, I hear ya." Angela then gets up.

I'll be in my room." She then walks away.

"We aren't fighting are we?" Malik asks.

"No, babe I understand." She flashes a fraudulent smile at him although but he knows she's upset.

A few minutes later Malik walks to the bathroom for a quick shower while she was in her walk-in closet. He gets dressed and comes into the bedroom. He finds her, with her back to the dresser wearing a black see-through housecoat that stops at her juicy caramel thighs. Malik looks into Angela's beautiful green eyes.

"So I take it we're not going to the club tonight." Malik says as Angela undoes the belt of her housecoat revealing her black laced bra and thongs. "You tell me." she says. Malik walks to her and places his hands on her hips kissing her soft lips teasingly. He kisses her on the side of her neck as she raises her thigh brushing his side lusting him more and more. "Oh Malik I want you." she says softly in his ear. He picks her up and lays her on the bed. Malik kisses her body on down to the depts holding her laced garment to the side, sending her mind into a fantastic fulfilled frenzy. Malik then enters Angela with a gentle ease slowly as she breathes and moans in his ear as he grinds. "Oh, I need you Malik, stay with me tonight." she says as he grinds more and more until they climax together. "I'm not going anywhere Angie." he breathes out as she holds on to him tightly.

A few weeks later, it is the end of summer. Malik is now pretty much done building his home in Tennessee. Confused, he has been contemplating moving back home. So he tells Angela that he needs a few days to clear his head. Angela, meanwhile, knows what's at stake. She just spends her time at work and at home. After a few days of not talking, Angela decides to pay Malik a visit. She pulls up into the parking lot. In an instant, her heart falls, when she sees Malik and a mysterious woman coming out of the apartment, laughing then hug. With Melissa not yet back from her vacation, Angela thinks the worst, then leaves. Later that evening, Malik pays Angela a visit. She answers the door, lets him in then lets him have it.

"You could've at least called, or is this how you do things?" she says.

"What?" Malik says all puzzled.

"I thought we meant something to each other. Maybe I was wrong." Malik still confused.

What are you talking-" She cuts him off with, "I saw her." Malik then realizes what this is about, but it's too late. By this time Angela is not in the mood for an explanation. All she knows is that Malik is walking out of her life, just like Derick. Malik tries to explain, but Angela's not listening. She then tells him to get out.

"Angela" he says.

"Just go, Malik!" she says. Malik, done trying as he looks at Angela then leaves.

After a couple of hours of contemplating on whether she over reacted or not, Angela goes to apologize. By this time Melissa is back at home. Melissa lets Angela in, as Angela tells her what happened. Melissa shakes her head and says, "Angie that was his baby sister Deitra. She just came back from Iraq." Melissa explains.

"Oh, I feel so stupid." she says to Melissa.

"Girl go find your man, I got Chris."

In a local bar not too far from the apartment sits Malik drinking shots of liquor as he contemplates leaving. A woman in the bar comes and sits next to him. "Hey daddy, what are you drinking? Want to get together and have a good time?" Out of nowhere a voice says, "No he would not!" Malik turns around and sees Angela looking as if she's ready to rip the woman in half. The woman gets up and staggers off mumbling gibberish as Angela looks with a mean look on her grill.

"Can we talk?" asks Angela.

"Yeah, sure." he says as Angela sits next to him.

"First of all I want to apologize for the way I over reacted. It's just that this turning point in our relationship is killing me. I don't want you to leave, because I don't want to lose you. You're the best thing that's ever happened to me and I love you."

"Ever since I fell in love with you, I've been beating myself up wondering what to do when we got to this point Angie. The truth is you got everything you need right here. You've got your family, your home and your career. I can't provide for you the type of life for you that you deserve Angie." Malik says as Angela eyes filled with tears. "So that's it huh, you just gonna walk out on me too?" she says.

"Angela I'm sorry." Malik attempts to hold her. Angela steps back shakes her head then turns and walk away.

It has now been a month since Malik broke up with Angela. He moved into his new home with his daughters. At times he sat alone staring out into space thinking about Angela and all the what ifs. He looked at the selfie that remained in his phone and wanted to call her, but decided that maybe he should just let go

On a Saturday afternoon Malik along with his dad, (brother) Sean, and Ray, are painting the last room in the house. Malik is carrying on yet another conversation about Angela. Finally Ray has had his fill of hearing about Angela.

"You know what? You need to put up a For Sale sign on this house, crank that raggedy ass truck up and go back to D.C. All you been talking about since you been back is Angela, ain't that right Mr. Jackson?" Ray says. Malik's dad and Sean laugh as they hear a knock at the door.

"I got it; it's probably your moma bringing us lunch." Mr. Jackson says. He opens the door and its Angela to his surprise. "Well I'll be John Brown, speak of the devil. How are you doing girl?" He says as he gives her a hug.

"I'm fine Mr. Jackson, how are you? Is Malik home?" she asks.

"Yeah, come on in." Mr. Jackson says as they walk inside.

"Well boy, you can quit telling all your sad stories now." Malik looks up, and feels like a child on Christmas Day when he sees Angela's face.

"Thank goodness you are here, cause he bout to drive us crazy." Sean says to Angela as she laughs. She then looks at Malik.

"Hi." she smiles. Malik was so surprised to see her as just stared, speechless. Mr. Jackson looked and says to Malik, "Don't just stand there, you been talking about her ever since you've been back." Malik gets up and gives her a big hug. They walk outside to the backyard.

"What happened to all the long hair?" Malik says of Angela about her new look.

"I cut it. You like it? Don't worry it'll grow back. I just decided to make a few changes." They sit in the gazebo in the backyard. She tells Malik that she gave everything back to her ex-husband; the car, the house, she even had the alimony discontinued. "Yeah, after you left I realized what was important, and that I really didn't need any of that." Angela says.

"So did you start at that new Doctor's Office yet?" Malik asked her.

"No, not yet, I wanted to weigh my options first." Angela says.

"So how's my main man Chris been doing?" He asks.

"Chris is fine, even though his father still won't come see him. He's fine."

That sucks ya know. Every child deserves to have a father in their lives." Malik says.

"Your right...which is why I came to see you." Angela says as she stands up, facing away from him as Malik starts looking all confused.

"You want me to become a father figure for Chris?" He asked her.

"You remember when you said to me that things happen for a reason?" Angela says to Malik.

"Yeah, and I've always have believed that." He says. Angela looks at Malik, taking her time.

"Malik, I'm pregnant. I just found out two weeks ago. I'm into my sixth week now." She says as Malik was speechless. "Well, aren't you gonna say something?" Angela asked.

"Angie, I don't know what to say baby I'm just so happy right now." He says, as he stands up, hugs her, and then holds her in his arms.

And just like that a new chapter began in Angela and Malik's life. One day, between their constant visits to each other, Malik proposed. Angela and Chris moved to Tennessee with Malik and his daughters. After giving birth to a son, ironically they named him what she called Malik that night she met him in the club, Malcolm. Business started to boom for Malik and his construction company. Angela opened her own family doctor's office in Memphis.

On a beautiful Saturday afternoon in the summer, they had a big wedding in their backyard. Angela's mom was in attendance along with Melissa (the maid of honor) and a few more of her relatives and friends. Three of Malik's groomsmen consisted of his brother Sean, his cousin Frank and of course Ray as the best man. Little Chris was the ring bearer while Malisha and Jasmine served as flower girls. It was a beautiful wedding on a lovely day. Angela and Malik had reached the epitome of happiness, thus more in each other they found how to mend a broken heart.

· · · · ·

A Flame Rekindled

It was a house party after the homecoming game. Sophomore guard, Jason Miller Scored 38 points and hit the game winning shot. Jason, along with his cousin Greg Miller, played college basketball. Of the two, Jason was the more, well- rounded dominate player, and was becoming a household name in college basketball. At this house party, Greg's girlfriend, freshmen Yvette Smith, and her best friend and fellow freshmen Felicia Hinckley, awaited Greg's arrival. Greg enters the party and comes over and talks to Yvette and Felicia. Jason, whom has aspirations to play in the professional basketball league, enters the party.

Jason Miller, all six foot, six inches of him, and now he's coming this way.

"Vette, I changed my mind, I can't do it. I'm bout to go." says a very nervous and shy Felicia as she attempts to walk away. Yvette holds her by the arm and says to her, "No you not! Come on Lisa, Jay really wants to meet you."

See several games before the homecoming game, Jason made only 5 of 15 shots and lost the ball, twice to the opposing team. This all because he couldn't keep his eyes off of this cute blue-eyed biracial chick sitting next to Yvette. Once he found out who she was, he asked Yvette to introduce him. That night at the party when Jason and Felicia met, they hit it off from the start. It was if they knew that night that they were meant for each other. It seemed as if time stood still, and that night would last forever, as they talked during and after the party.

Time went on and things began to get serious for them. In his senior year of college, Jason sat out with a damaged knee. Also during that same year, Felicia Hinckley became Felicia Miller, as Jason and she got married and moved in a small apartment. They didn't have much, but they had each other, and to them that was all they needed. The following year, Jason, in his final year of eligibility, damaged his other knee. Though the damage was done physically, it was severe mentally, considering a year ago he was being scouted to play in the pros. With his dreams now shattered, Jason was on a downward spiral, and all Felicia could do was watch. He was so caught up in feeling sorry for himself, that he wasn't there when Felicia needed him. Her father whom was a lawyer for the city's top firm passed away, the man who Felicia patterned herself after. After watching Jason drown himself in self-pity, Felicia left D.C. and transferred to a law school in Baltimore.

It has now been five years since their divorce or since they laid eyes on each other. Jason got his act together. He is now a chairman for one of the largest financial businesses in D.C., Whitfield. He never fully went away from basketball. In his spare time he serves as Greg's assistant coach for a local high school. Jason has become a big role model to one of his players in particular, Felicia's nephew, Dontrell Hinckley. Jason eventually got back in the dating game, but he's never had another serious relationship due of the way he handled his first marriage.

Felicia works for a firm and is one of the city's most sought after lawyers. Felicia is involved in a serious relationship with Ron Harris, a well-known lawyer on the verge of being recognized for his achievements by the city of Baltimore. Felicia has also been back and forth, visiting her best friend Yvette whom is married to Greg and has three children. On a down note, Yvette has been stricken with brain cancer and is in the fight for her life.

One night after a long conversation with Greg on the phone, Felicia prepares for bed. She lies in bed thinking about Yvette hoping she'd be okay. Felicia falls into a deep sleep. She opens her eyes and notices that she's in a hospital bed. She looks to her left and it's none other than Yvette sitting in a rocking chair holding a baby. 'This is all so strange' Felicia thought.

"Vette, what are you doing? Why aren't you in bed?" asks Felicia.

"Girl I'm fine now. Here, here's your baby since you're up now. It's okay to use mine" Yvette says to her.

"Baby" Felicia says with a puzzled look on her face. She was trying her best to make sense of all this, as Yvette gives her the child. The doorbell rings.

DING!

"Looks like you've got company." Yvette says as she answers the door. "It's your husband." she says as she looks at Felicia and smiles. The gentleman enters the room. Felicia, already astound about the baby, is now even more so at the man whom has just entered the room.

"Jay!" Felicia says.

"Well, you've been asking me about him long enough, now he's right here. Talk to him." The doorbell rings again.

DING!

"I better leave you two alone, I know y'all have a lot to talk about. Besides, they're out there waiting on me." Yvette says as she goes to the door, looks back at Felicia, Jason, and the baby and smile. She opens the door. A bright blinding light burst through the door, shinning so bright, Felicia holds up her arm in an attempt to block the light.

She awakens to find the sun shining in her face through the curtain. She then sits up in her bed trying to gather herself from this realistic dream she just had. As she sits there, the doorbell rings.

DING!

Felicia answers the door, it's Ron. She greets him and lets him in. "What brings you here so early this morning?" she asks. "I had a couple of tickets for that play and I was hoping after you finish your big case today, we could go out tonight." He says. "Yeah, sure." she says. As they talk a little more, the telephone rings. Felicia answers it, sits down, and holds her other hand over her mouth in disbelief. "No! no, no, God no!" she says, crying as she hangs up. "Baby what is it?" asks Ron, as he sits and put his arm around her. Taking a minute to catch her breath, Felicia says, "Vette... She, she's gone, she's gone."

Felicia battles through a long day that seemed to take forever. She holds back all of the sadness inside as she fights her case. With her five foot, nine inch slender frame, Felicia paces the courtroom floor rocking her beige pin-stripe pants suit and open-toe stilettoes. She emulated her father in the best way she knew how. This is what defines her, when the chips are stacked against her, she comes out fighting. After winning her case she goes home, packs her things then heads to D.C.

Felicia goes over to Greg and Yvette's home where their families are all gathered. She goes through and speaks to family members of both sides. She runs into her ex's parents before she comes upon Greg. She has a few encouraging words for Greg. She then goes out back talking with other family members and sees Jason. It's been five years since their divorce or since they've seen each other. Though she sometimes would ask Yvette about him, she never really made an attempt to talk to him, because she was trying to let go. She often wondered what would happen once they finally saw each other again. 'It's been five years, a lot has changed. Besides I'm with Ron now' Felicia thought to herself. As Jason talks to one of the family members, he looks over and locks eyes with Felicia for a brief second. They finally make their way towards each other with mixed emotions. Jason plays it cool with a little hug as he speaks to Felecia.

"Hey, how are you doing?" Felicia, feeling like she could just melt in his arms, but plays it cool as well.

"I'm good Jay, I'm good. Wow, look at you Mr. Suit and tie. I just talked with your mom and dad inside."

"So how long have you been in town?" he asks.

"I've only been here for like an hour or so. See I had to finish up a case earlier today, I came soon as I could."

Jason and Felicia talk for a while. He then tells her that he is going to keep the children since Greg still has a lot of guest. Felicia then says, "If you want, I can keep Sierra, while both of the boys stay with you." Jason agrees and is about to leave as he says to Felicia, "You look great Lisa. It was really nice seeing you."

Jason is now at home babysitting the boys. He plays a video game with them before putting them to bed. He then goes into his bedroom to check his e-mail. As he does so, the doorbell rings. Felicia is at the door along with Sierra. "Hey Jay, she was having trouble sleeping and wanted to come over with her brothers." Jason lets them in and escorts them to the room where the boys are. Felicia sits with her until she falls asleep. As Jason finishes reading his e-mail, Felicia comes back to the front where Jason is.

"Well I finally got her off to sleep, poor baby." says Felicia, as she notices an old familiar photograph of her and Jason on his shelf.

"Yeah, that's got to be tough on them." says Jason. He shuts down his computer.

"You have a nice home here Jay." she says as she makes her way to the door.

"Thanks, you know you don't have to leave so soon. You could stay a minute if you want." Felicia stands at the door with a look that says 'I don't know about this'.

"Please?" he asks as she ponders a moment.

"Oh what the heck" she says as she sits down on the sofa. They do some catching up as Felicia tells Jason about her long stressful day.

"Sounds like you could use a glass of this yourself." he says referring to the wine he was drinking.

"No thanks I'd better not. The way I feel I may just crash right here on your sofa."

"I wouldn't have a problem with that." he says.

"Yeah you wouldn't, but how are you going to explain me to your girlfriend?" she asks, then mockingly says, "See baby what had happened was…" as they both laugh.

"So how've you been holding up through this? Cause after all you two were inseparable?"

"I'm fine Jay, really. I just couldn't believe it when Greg called me this morning. Vette was always trying to make me laugh and not worry about her even when she was at her worst." Felicia reminisces with her voice cracking and tears in her eyes. Jason gets closer to her. He places his arm around her then rubs her back as she says she's fine. She takes a minute before changing the subject.

"I hear you're quite the coach these days."

"Yeah, Greg and I are doing pretty good. Your nephew has got some skills, he's nice. In fact he's on my summer league team. If you happen to be in town when we're playing one night, come by and see us."

"Okay, I will." she smiles.

"So how's business?" he asks.

"I've been doing fine. The business is good, even so that the guys at my father's old firm wants me to come home and work for them but, I've come accustom to Baltimore." She says. After talking for a while she then gets up and walks to the door.

"Well Jay, I'd better go, it's getting late and I have to get back home tomorrow."

"So soon?" he asks.

"Yeah, but I'll be back Tuesday or Wednesday."

"Tell you what; I'll give you my number if it's cool."

"It's cool Jay." They then exchange phone numbers as Jason walks her outside to her car, gives her a hug and says goodnight.

The weekend goes by as Jason gets back to work on Monday. On his way home from work Jason gets a call from Felicia's sister Denise. She tells Jason that Dontrell had an argument with her boyfriend, walked out, and now she doesn't know where he is. Jason, whom has become close with Dontrell since coaching him, finds him at the first place he decides to look, at the park shooting basketball. Jason gets out of his car in his casual attire, looking as if he's ready for a photo shoot for GQ magazine. He walks onto the court and begins shooting ball with Dontrell.

"D, what's going on? You got Niecey worried sick looking for you." Jason says.

"Uncle Jay, she don't care about nothing but what ole stupid Marcus say. Every time she gets some ole dumb boyfriend me and Alicia (Dontrell's little sister) always got to listen to them." Dontrell explains as Jason holds the ball.

"D, y'all may not agree with everything Niecey tells you, but she **is** your mother and I want you to always respect that ok."

"Yes sir." says a resentful Dontrell. Jason then jokingly says to him, "Cause you don't want me to come up in here getting on that head of yours." Dontrell thinks to when he was little and says to Jason in a serious manner, "Sometimes I use to wish you was my daddy, Uncle Jay. Why you and Aunt Felicia break up anyway?" Jason answers in the most honest way he knows how. "D, sometimes things just happen. I don't know why, they just do. Anyway, come on so I can take you home alright." They then leave.

The next day Jason was in an important meeting at work. It seems that he is the leading candidate to relocate and head the company's expansion in Miami. They advise him to take a few days to think it over and give a response. After the meeting, Jason stands in his office looking out the window at the city that he's loved his whole life. His quiet time is quickly interrupted by his nosey secretary Mary. She notifies him of a call and as usual they go back and forth as she adds a little extra. "Jason you have a call on line one. She says it's from a Mrs. Miller, but it don't sound nothing like your moma." she says. "Mary, don't make me fire you. You're doing too much and the unemployment line is just screaming your name." he says. "Well what do you want me to tell her." "Woman if you don't transfer my call." he says as she then transfers the call to his desk. To his surprise it's Felicia whom informs him that she's now back in town and that she was really calling to say thanks for talking to her nephew.

"Just because we're divorce doesn't mean we have to act a certain way, besides Dontrell and Alicia still call me Uncle Jay whenever they see me." Jason says.

"Well, **you** were their favorite uncle." says a sarcastic Felicia, whom only has one sibling.

"I was their only uncle." says Jason as they share a laugh. They talk a little while longer then Felicia says, "Well, if I don't see you around today, I'll see you at the memorial service tomorrow ok." They hang up then Jason carries on with his work.

After work, Jason goes by the mall to his favorite department store of casual wear. He finds a suit to wear to the funeral. He approaches the counter, where he runs into, none other than Felicia, who in turn was doing a little shopping as well. They speak as she digs in her purse for her credit card Jason in turn gives his credit card to the clerk.

"I got it." Jason says.

"Jay, you don't have to do this." Felicia responds.

"Oh, it's no big deal Leese, I got it." Jason says. The clerk ,Katrina, looks on curiously. "You two must know each other?" she asks as she swipes Jason's card. Jason says to Katrina, "Oh yeah, we go way back, we're the best of friends." Felicia smiles and shakes her head. Seeing Jason pay for $200 of merchandise for Felicia. "Girlfriend you got to tell me your secret. I need me a friend like this." Katrina says to Felicia as she smiles.

On their way out of the store as they're about to part ways, Jason asks Felicia if he could take her out to dinner. Felicia on the verge of yet another slow yes as Jason pleads. "Come on Lisa, just this once. Please!" "Alright" Felicia says, knowing all along she wasn't going to say no to him. Just like it was when they were married. What Jason wants, Jason gets. No matter how upset with him she was, she always gave in, because she knew in her heart he'd do the same for her.

Felicia does some bonding with her mother and sister. Later that night at their mother's house, Denise helps Felicia make final preparations for her dinner date by doing her hair. Jason arrives outside.

"It sounds like your ride is out there. Who did you say you were going out with?" asks Denise.

"Oh just an old friend from college." says Felicia, whom goes quickly to get her purse before Jason gets out. While Felicia acts suspiciously as she rushes, Denise curiously peeks out of the window and sees a black Dodge Charger underneath the streetlight.

"Somebody's got a nice car." Denise says then it dawns on her as to whose car it is. She opens her mouth with a big smirk, and puts her hands on her hips and says, "Trying to rekindle that flame huh."

"No I'm not!" says Felicia while telling Denise to keep it down. "We're just going out to eat Miss nosey. Tell momma I'll be back soon." she says. Felicia heads to the door as Denise continues to tease her about Jason. "Girl bye" Felicia says as she heads out.

Jason wanted to surprise Felicia as to where they would be dinning out. They rode until they came upon this place called Moody's Rib Shack. It's a place where they use to hang out with Greg and Yvette, during their college years. It is also where Jason proposed to Felicia. As they dine they share laughs on some good memories.

While there, Felicia sees an old next door neighbor named Angela at the diner, so she walks over to say hi.

"Hey Angie, how've you been?" Felicia says as they embrace each other with a big hug   .

"I'm blessed Lisa. I've moved to Tennessee, I'm getting married, and I'll be starting my own doctor's office as Dr. Angela Jackson." she says.

"That's great Angie."

"Thanks, so you and he (Jason) back together huh?"

"Oh, no, I'm just in town for Yvette's funeral and we were just doing some catching up."

"Oh okay, that's sweet. I remember you used to be so crazy about him. The funny thing about love is that if it's real, **you** know it deep down inside. Girl I don't know what I'd do without Malik. Anyway don't let me interrupt you guys, was good seeing you Lisa." Felicia then continues her diner date with Jason. So after dinner, Jason pulls back in front of Felicia's mother's house. As they get closer to her mother's, 'Lady in my life' by Michael Jackson comes on the radio.

"Oh my god, this is crazy" she says. "What?" Jason asks. Felicia turns up the radio. "You use to sing this to me all the time." Felicia says as they reminisce. He pulls into the driveway and shuts off the engine as they continue talking. "So are you gonna answer my question or what Jay? Why are you being so nice to me?" she asks. Jason takes a deep breath and exhales. "A few years ago I felt like I was on top of the world when I was about to go pro. When I fell, I fell hard. I gave up, and it cost me everything, including the best wife a guy could ever ask for. Felicia I am so sorry I hurt you. I just want you to forgive me." "Aw Jay it's alright. All of that is behind us now. Besides I already forgave you." Just to hear her say that was like a weight that he toted for years being lifted of his shoulders. They hug and are about to say goodnight. "I really enjoyed hanging out with you tonight." she says. She then kisses him on the cheek. Jason leans towards Felicia and presses his lips against hers. He kisses her deeply and rolls his tongue as she lustfully moans. Felicia gets caught up in the moment holding on to Jason as tightly as he held her. Their moment was then interrupted by her cell.

"It's Ron" she exhales. "Jay, I got to go." She then gets out of the car just before she answers the phone. As she goes inside. Jason watches that sexy little walk in which he's always admired.

Thursday evening, two days before Yvette's funeral, a few friends and family members again gather at Greg's home after a memorial service. Among the group of people, mingling separate, are Jason and Felicia. As they prepare for the funeral and socialize, Felicia somewhat avoids Jason due to what took place the night before. It's not that she doesn't want to talk to him it's just that she doesn't want to ruin her relationship with Ron. Several times Jason approaches Felicia, and tries to talk to her. Each time he tries, she cuts him short, as if she has something to do. This goes on for a while. Jason finally gets the chance to talk to her alone. He walks over to her.

"Are you gonna ignore me all night?" Jason says.

"We should not have let that happened last night. I'm seeing someone now Jay." says Felicia.

"It was just a kiss Lisa, besides you felt that last night just as much as I did." Jason says.

"Oh really, Jay, stop pretending you know me so well because you don't"

"Then why didn't you stop me?" he asks as a speechless Felicia folded her arms and roll her eyes.

"I thought so. You know what Lisa, forget it. Maybe its best if we go back to just staying away from each other…What the hell was I thinking anyway huh." Jason about to leave when Felicia grabs his arm. "Jay!" As he snatches his arm away then walks off.

Greg comes outside looking for Jason, Felicia tells him that something must have come up and that Jason had to leave.

"You know, It's good to see you two talking again. Jay took it kind of hard when you two split up. It took him a minute before he started back dating. I remember when he went to Baltimore to find you." Felicia suspiciously looks at Greg.

"Came to Baltimore for me? What are you talking about Greg? Jay never came to Baltimore for me."

"Sure he did. When you finished college he set out to go find you and bring you back home. He asked Vette not to say anything because he wanted to surprise you. He said he got all the way there and thought about all the hell he'd put you through and that he just wanted you to be happy. Anyway it's great seeing you two talk." Greg then walks over and talks with his in-laws. Felicia thinks about what Greg said as she then leaves.

Felicia arrives back at her mother's home. With a lot on her mind, Felicia tells her mother that she just going to go lie down. She goes into her room, sits on her bed, lies on her back then stares into space. Felicia thinks that maybe she was a little hard on Jason she decides to give him a call. After she gets no answer, she leaves a message on his voice mail. She lies in her bed awaiting his call until she falls asleep.

The following evening, inclement weather sets in and lightning flashes across the sky as if it would storm at any given moment. After a long tireless day of conducting meetings, Jason comes home. Instead of unwinding from his long day, Jason gets on his computer and brushes up on a few things for next week. Minutes turn into hours before he's done and can officially say it's Friday. He takes a long shower before relaxing in front of the television. While watching television, someone knocks at the door. He opens the door a little to find Felicia to his surprise.

"May I come in?" she says. Jason opens the door up so that she may. Felicia comes in looking irresistible as ever. "Why haven't you returned my calls Jay?" she asks. Jason closes the door behind her.

"Oh, so we only talk when you're good and ready huh?" Jason says aggressively. Felicia pauses in an attempt to calm the situation as she says to Jason, "Look Jay, I didn't come here to fight alright. It's just that I've got so much going on right now."

"I'm sorry if I came on a little strong the other night. It's just that I've missed you so much Leese." Jason says to her. Felicia, being sincere, says to Jason, "Jay, I never really wanted to leave you like I did." "Yeah I know but I didn't leave you much of a choice either did I?" says Jason. As their conversation deepens, the butterflies in Felicia's stomach flutter. She then asks, "So, do you ever think of how things would've turned out if you and I could've fixed things?" Jason then looks at Felicia with seriousness and answers in a weary voice, "All the time."

Felicia then holds on to Jason as if she never wants to let go. Thunderous claps and the sound of precipitation get stronger by the minute, as does the affection Felicia has for Jason. Indulging the moment, they begin kissing as if it's their last time. While kissing, they undress, leaving a trail of clothing all the way to the bedroom piece by piece. In the bedroom Jason undoes Felicia's bra freeing her voluptuous breast as he caresses them. He kisses her neck as she breathes heavily. "Oh Jay" Jason eases inside of Felicia as he looks into her deep blue eyes. He begins thrusting her as she holds him tightly. Deep into their passionate evening they lay on the bed as his chest is pressed against her back. Jason holds her hips, thrusting her harder and faster. "Oh Jason, you're making me. You're making me. Ah!!"

Daylight breaks on the morning of the funeral, as Felicia and Jason lay in each other's arms. The two are soon awaken by the doorbell. "Shit! Who is that this early in the morning?" says Jason. They begin stumbling all over each other, trying to get their clothes on. "I'm coming!" says Jason, as he creeps to the door's peephole to see who it is. "It's Greg!" he whispers across the room to Felicia, as she picks up her shoes and clothing and race to the bathroom.

Soon as the coast is clear Jason opens the door. "What's up man, come on in." he says. "I was just um, yeah. You know.

So what brings you here so early this morning." Without saying a word, Greg enters and walks over to the sofa. Felicia enters the room. Greg sits down, stares into space and sighs. "This is it. Last time I'm gonna to see my wife." he says as his voice cracks as the tears begin to fall. "Why her? Vette ain't never done nothing to hurt nobody." Felicia sits next to Greg to comfort him as she starts to cry. Jason can only stand there and watch his cousin suffer a lost as tears stream down his face as well.

Around noon on this same hot summer's day, a host of family and friends join to celebrate the life of Yvette Miller. On the front pew is the family she left behind. A row back sits Felicia alongside Ron, whom is in attendance for her support. About half way through the program Jason comes to the podium to share a few words. Wiping away tears, Jason speaks highly of Yvette and of lasting friendships. After Jason speaks Felicia comes up. She expresses a few words on behalf of her best friend. She then delivers a powerful and touching version of 'His eye is on the sparrow'. As she sang there wasn't a dry eye in the church.

After the funeral, family and friends gather one last time. Jason talks with ex-girlfriend, Nichelle Perez, whom also attended the funeral. Felicia can't help but notice the floozy in the tight skirt that Jason is with. She tries not to let curiosity get the best of her, but can't help it. As Jason and Nichelle talk, Felicia comes over to introduce Ron and to say goodbye.

"I loved your song. Muy simpatico... It was nice." Nichelle says to Felicia with her Spanish accent as the guys step aside and start to carry on about basketball.

"Thank you." Felicia says to Nichelle.

"It's nice finally meeting you. I heard so much about you when Jason and I were involved." Nichelle says as Felicia looks at her curiously. "He still loves you Chicka." Nichelle says as Felicia looks over at Jason. "Well, I have to go to work now. Again, it was nice meeting you." Nichelle then says as she leaves.

"Oh okay, it was nice meeting you too." Felicia says. Nichelle then walks over to Jason gives him a hug. He thanks her for coming as Felicia looks on. Jason then continues talking with Ron and Felicia. Ron gets an important call and excuses himself, leaving Felicia to say goodbye to Jason as they do so before parting ways.

Weeks go by since Felicia and Jason had rekindled their friendship. Emptiness is the word that best describes the emotion in Felicia's heart where happiness should be. The life in which she has come to know now feels distant and strange all of a sudden.

The city of Baltimore is about to hold its annual banquet honoring some of its very own. Ron Harris is among this year's honorees. Felicia is at home getting dressed for the ceremony. While getting dressed, she receives a call from Jason. She immediately puts everything on hold as she joyously talks with Jason.

"You know Lisa, about the other night, what happened between us" he says.

"Look Jay, what happened, happened. I just wish I didn't feel so guilty about it every time I'm with Ron." For a brief moment it is quiet on both ends of the phone line. Jason then breaks the news to her about his job opportunity in Miami.

Oh, well, yeah if it's what you want. You should do it. I'm sure Miami's would be great." Felicia says, hoping that he would reconsider. Jason on the other end didn't get the answer in which he was seeking either.

"Thanks Leese, it was great talking to you. I'll see you around okay." he says.

The lights come on and the stage is set as the banquet begins. Felicia sits next to Ron watching others accept their own prestigious award. The spotlight is now on Ron Harris for his services to the community. He is introduced then is escorted to the stage by Felicia. Ron gives an outstanding thanks speech and then introduces his leading lady to the audience. Next he does the unthinkable. Ron calls Felicia to the podium and proposes to her as the crowd looks on. Felicia approaches the podium as she is taken by surprise.

"Wow Ron, I don't know what to say." She pauses for a moment, searches her feelings then speaks from her heart. "You know these past two years with you have been really wonderful Ron. You are an amazing guy and truly deserving of the recognition bestowed upon you tonight. It would be an honor to be your wife, but I can't accept." She steps away from the microphone "I'm sorry." She then steps off stage in the back and leaves the building.

Like a thief in the night going unnoticed, Felicia drives though the bright lights and busy streets of Baltimore. She drives onto her very own safe haven, her mother's house. A concerned Mrs. Hinckley answers the door.

"Felicia, child its two o'clock in the morning what's wrong?" Felicia just shakes her head. "Come on in." Felicia comes in and sits at the dining room table as her mother makes her favorite, hot chocolate. "So are you going to tell me what's bothering you?" asks Mrs. Hinckley.

"Ron asked me to marry him tonight. I just couldn't say yes moma." Mrs. Hinckley sits down and gives Felicia a briefing in Mother's intuition.

"I knew you weren't going to marry him."

"Why do you say that?"

Oh it ain't always easy to put something past your mother, Felicia Lajoyce Hinckley. You and your sister ought to know that by now. The moment I saw you and Jay talking and how you've been acting around here lately, I knew that poor boy was in trouble." she says as Felicia listens. "I remember your father wasn't exactly fun of Jay at first, but you were just as stubborn as he was and never gave up on what you wanted. Yeah you are your father's daughter alright." Mrs. Hinckley gets up from the table. "Well I'm about go back to bed. I'll see you in the morning cause I'm not the one you need to be talking to." Mrs. Hinckley says, giving Felicia a hint.

The next day Felicia along with her sister and mother enjoy one of Dontrell's summer league games. During the course of the game, Dontrell shows off his skill as a basketball player. Jason paces back and forth in front of his team's bench, looking dapper in his dress shirt and slacks. He yells at the officials over calls and gets onto his team for slacking on defense. Jason coaches with the same passion and intensity in which he once played, not quitting until the last second ticked off the clock.

It was a hard fought well-played game, but on this day the victory goes to the opposing team. After the game, Jason talks to his team. He gives them a few words of encouragement and tells them how proud he was of them and the way they played. They say a quick word of prayer and leave the gym. As Jason makes it to his car he hears a familiar voice. "You need to calm down out there coach." He turns around and sees Felicia.

"You got a minute?"

Yeah, what's up?"

"Jay I haven't exactly been honest with you or myself for that matter. And I wouldn't blame you if you choose to leave, but just hear me out first. All this about me being happy, I mean I thought I was, but being with you again made me realize that no matter what, my heart will always belong to you. You're my soul mate Jay and I love you. So if you decide to go to Miami I understand, I'll just have to deal with it." She waits on Jason to respond but he does not. Jason opens his car door as Felicia starts to walk away.

"Hey Lisa, you still make that Italian chicken casserole?" he says to her. Felicia looks at him and nods her head. "How about bringing some over to my place around eight o'clock."

"Okay" she smiles.

Later Felicia arrives at Jason's home with her casserole. She walks up to the door where she finds a sticky note with a rose petal attached to it simply reads 'Follow the trail'. She opens the door and sees a trail of rose petals that lead to the kitchen, where she finds a bouquet of roses, a poem, and a second note instructing her to place the casserole in the oven that's already set to warm and to look in the refrigerator. In the refrigerator she finds a glass of wine. She takes a sip and continues to follow the trail of rose petals and now along with candles into the hall as they lead to the bathroom. She opens the door and sees rose petals all on the floor and candles placed along the sink counter and around a hot bubble filled tub. On the sink counter is note next to a remote control. The note simply reads, Just press play. Marvin Gaye's 'Til Tomorrow' softly plays as Felicia undresses and gets into the tub.

After a relaxing bath, Jason joins Felicia in the bedroom. As she lay on the bed Jason massages her body down with oil. He starts kissing his way down her body to the depts. She heavily exhales and breathes out his name as he takes her mind beyond the point of ecstasy. Jason then lies on his back next to her as she strokes him gently. Felicia then straddles and eases her way down on him as Jason holds her at the waist. Each swirl of her hips gets more and more intense. The very thought of him inside of her turns her on more and more. Her heart races as she grinds faster and faster and digs into his chest as she climaxes. He sits up and she kisses him on the cheek as they hold each other tightly.

Within the coming weeks Felicia takes up her father's old colleagues on their offer to join their firm in D.C. Jason declines the job offer in Miami. Though he did not take the job, he did however take a few business trips to Miami to help get things started (with Felicia at his side of course). Spending more and more time together Jason and Felicia rekindled their love for each other. And on a random night, in the middle of a dinner date at an upscale restaurant, Jason proposed to Felicia again. He vowed to make her the number one priority in his life. She accepted without a second thought. This time around a more mature Jason showed that his whole world revolved around Felicia.

Jason and Felicia remarried and started a family of two sons named Jason and Jared. On the night after giving birth to their third child, a tired Felicia fell into a deep sleep. She started to wake up in her hospital bed. As she began to open her eyes up, she looked to her left. And for a brief moment the image that she thought she saw was that of an old friend. When she rubbed her eyes and was fully awake, she realized it was her mother in a rocking chair next to her bed holding their baby girl. Felicia then hears a knock at the door.

"Looks like you got company." Mrs. Hinckley says. Felicia gives this eerie look as if she's been here before as Jason comes in with the boys and his mom and dad. Their parents talk as boys meet their baby sister. Felicia tells Jason about this dream she had the night Yvette died. She tells him that she specifically remembers Yvette saying that it was okay to use hers.

"I wonder what she meant" Felicia says.

"So what are you all going to name her?" Mrs. Hinckley asks. Felicia and Jason look at each other as the answer to her question unfolds.

We'll name her Yvette" Felicia says as Jason smiles.

・ ・ ・ ・ ・

What Happened in The Bayou

O It was just another hot summer's day in the city of Atlanta. It is the end of the day for some, as for police officer Frank Battle it is the beginning of shift. Officer Frank Battle, a bit on the rough side cowboyish, yet one of Atlanta's finest on the force. After roll call and a shift briefing, Frank is approached by one of his superiors, Sergeant Timothy McCoy.

"Hey, Battle, Lieutenant Henderson needs to see you in her office."

"Yes sir" says Frank. As Sergeant McCoy walks off Frank is then teased by his friend Officer Tony Wilson. "Damn, Battle, you stay in trouble," he says. Frank, knowing that this is true, can only smile as he heads to the Lieutenant's office. Frank walks into Lieutenant Ronda Henderson's office.

"Hey Lieu, you need to see me?" he asks.

"Yeah, Battle. Come on in" says Lieutenant Henderson. Frank closes the door and takes a seat in front of her desk. She pulls out a manila folder, places it on her desk and opens it up. She then pushes her eyeglasses up on her nose then does her everyday ritual and puts on her chap stick. Lieutenant Henderson looks at his file. Though she's only nine years older, she begins to scold Frank as a mother would a child.

"Officer Battle, Officer Battle." she says with her Brooklyn accent. Frank can only look with the guilty face, thinking about the patrol car he wrecked last week in a high-speed chase.

"Officer Battle, you know that your evaluation is coming up right?"

Yes Ma'am." Frank says unenthused like.

"Oh okay. I just don't want you to be surprised, because it's not looking too good for you right now Mr. Battle. Of course you already know that, right?"

"Yes Ma'am"

Lieutenant Henderson then gives Frank a little encouragement. "Battle, you're a great officer, that's why Captain Gibson and I push you so hard. You're a great asset to this precinct. I'd highly recommend you for sergeant, but you are like some loose cannon. You're just like your Uncle John. Oh, by the way how's he enjoying retirement?"

"He's doing good." says Frank. Then she speaks to him, not as a Lieutenant, but as a friend. "Listen, you need to quit trying to do it all by yourself. That's what your team is for. At the rate you're going you won't get to see your retirement. You got a lot people here who really care about you. **I** care about you, and I'm not just saying that because of what happened after the New Year's party last year. So help me, if anybody finds out about that"

"Come on Lieu, I wouldn't put that out there."

"I'm just saying. Anyways after tonight I'm placing you on two weeks leave with pay. I recommend you take this time off and get plenty of rest and unwind. Ok."

"Yes ma'am"

"That's all for now Officer Battle. Have a great night and be safe."

When Frank leaves out of the Lieutenants' office he is greeted by fellow officers Rodney Black, Keisha Thomas (KT), and Marshall Boatwright.

"What's going on K.T. Boatwright and Black?"

"Battle, what's up man? She didn't chew it all off did she?" Officer Black says. Officer Thomas joins in, "Turn around and let me see if you got anything left back there." They laugh as Lieutenant Henderson steps out of her office with her coffee cup in hand.

"Alright now! Let's get to work, we're not paying you all to stand around and kick the bobo." All officers disperse to begin their tour of duty.

With his car totaled, Frank is now paired to ride with Officer Alexis Watts. They are about to get into the patrol car.

"Hey Watts, you want me to drive?"

She gives him the look and says, "Oh Hell No! Lieu said that you better not even look at the steering wheel in this car."

"Damn, that's messed up Watts. I thought we were cool."

"Just get in the car."

"Now, Watts, before we leave"

"Yes I'm wearing my bulletproof vest Battle."

"I'm just trying to look out for you...Lexie"

Whatever, and quit calling me that." She says with a smirk. They begin patrolling and stop at the local convenient store as Frank does at the beginning of each shift. Frank goes in gets his coffee just the way he likes it, straight without sugar or cream. As usual he has to flirt with the cashier, Cynthia, before exiting the store. When Frank comes back out to the car he is greeted by his uncle, John MacArthur Battle. A former cop himself, John (or Uncle Mac as Frank calls him) has always been like a father to Frank. John teases with Officer Watts then, as usual, he gives a bit of advice to Frank.

"Hey son, be careful out there. It's not like it was when I was on the force. A lot has changed now."

Alright Uncle Mac, I got you."

Frank and Officer Watts begin patrolling the city of Atlanta. As they talk she asks, "So what are you gonna do on your time off Battle?"

"I don't know. Probably go to Memphis and hang out with my cousin Sean."

"Oh, in that case, there ain't no telling where you two outlaws may end up. My girl Tosha wants me to go out of town with her for a wedding. I'm not sure if I'm going though." They continue their conversation as they patrol the city, having just another night at work.

While off from work, Frank spends time with family and friends. As his time off approaches the end, Frank and Sean set out for a weekend in New Orleans. They reach their destination on a Friday afternoon and stop at a gas station. Frank goes in to pay for the gas and get some beer. As he walks down the aisle, he sees this strikingly beautiful lady named Natosha Batiste.

Natohsa is your everyday good girl whom does not like to take chances. She's a bit on the shy side, not to mention, in an on again- off again relationship with Mr. Wrong. Natosha, a native of New Orleans happens to be in town to attend her brother's wedding.

Frank can't help but notice how her painted finger and toe nails compliment her beautiful brown skin, or how her short hair sets off the sun dress and sandals she wore. Frank walks past her and has to look back and get a double take

"Hi," she says as her dimples start to show from her smile. Frank is so in awe that he thinks out loud.

"Damn!"

"Excuse me?" she says.

"Oh, I'm sorry. Hi." He quickly snaps out of it. She smiles and walks to the register as Frank catches a glimpse of her work that sundress like Serena in a tennis skirt. Frank makes it back outside. As Sean pumps gas, Frank notices Natosha can't seem to get in her car. So he walks over.

"Hey, you need some help."

"Yeah, I locked my keys in my car." she says embarrassedly.

"I can get them out for you."

Frank gets a wire hanger and immediately begins to work on getting into her car. While working on getting her door open, they are formally introduced. Natosha catches a glimpse of Frank's broad shoulders and big muscles as he works the wire hanger into her car. They carry on a running conversation. She explains that she is on her way to her brother's wedding rehearsal. In no time flat Frank has the door open.

"There you go."

"Thank you. What do I owe you?"

"Oh nothing, one thing I was taught…. never leave a beautiful woman in distress."

"Well, I don't know how to repay you, but thanks again Frank."

"Tell you what; my cousin and I are here on vacation for the weekend. I would like it if I could see you again somewhere." he smiles. She thinks about it for a second.

"Well later on, a couple of my girlfriends were going to take me the Spoken Word Lounge." she explains and gives Frank directions. They then exchange numbers and bid one another farewell.

The night is young at the Spoken Word Lounge. The crowd is enjoying the jazzy sounds of the live band playing. Natosha is in the company of two childhood friends (twins) Roxanne and Rosalind Debasse. The ladies sit at their table having drinks and reminiscing. Frank and Sean walk through the club until Frank spots Natosha, baiting for him to come over. Roxanne, the more outspoken of the twins asks, "Tosha, who is that?"

"This guy I met earlier."

"Oooh girl, he looks nice, and he's got muscles." She gawks as Natosha taps her on the leg underneath the table as the guys approach.

"Hi, did you have any trouble finding it?"

"Not at all, your directions were right on point."

"Great. Frank these are my friends Roxy and Roz."

"Ladies, this is my cousin Sean." As they take a seat.

"So where are you guys from?" Roxanne asks.

"Memphis." Sean says. He and Roxanne take all the focus off of Frank and Natosha and go back and forth flirting.

"What brings yall to New Orleans?"

"We're just two bachelors out looking for a good time. We work hard and play hard." he says and winks at Roxanne.

"What kind of work do y'all do?"

"Well I do construction, my brother and I run our own business. Frank here is cop."

"Oooh, so you pretty good with your hands huh." Roxanne says.

"Baby, I'm the best." Sean says as Rosalind looks at Franks and says "Don't mind her."

"Well he's not making it any better." Frank laughs. After a few minutes of getting acquainted, Roxanne goes to the ladies room as the guys head to the bar to buy a round of drinks. While everyone else is away Rosalind and Natosha have a heart to heart, being that they were always so close.

"They seem like a lot of fun. You better claim that Frank before Roxy does. You know she don't play." She then asks, "So how are things going in Atlanta, Miss LPN? Are you still with Mike or what?"

"We had another big fight and broke up right before I left."

Is he still putting he hands on you?" Rosalind asks as Natosha looks away and refuses to answer.

"Girl, if Terry (Natosha's brother) ever finds out, he's coming straight to Atlanta and kick his ass. Natosha, you were one of the smartest people I ever met. Why do you settle for less? You can do so much better than him." Rosalind says as the guys make it back from the bar. A few minutes later the band finishes playing as the DJ starts. Sean goes on to the dance floor with the twins. Frank is still in conversation with Natosha, making her laugh.

"So are you going to dance with me or are you going to let your friends have all the fun?" he smiles. She then gets up and heads to the dance floor with him. The very next song comes on is Juvenile's Back That Ass Up. "Oh No" Natosha, embarrassingly attempts to leave the dance floor. "I'm not going to let you off that easy, come on." Frank takes her by the hand. Natosha, in her well fitted jeans, begins to get into the song and back it up on Frank. After they dance they come back to their seats. The MC of the evening comes on stage. He asks if there are any poets in the club that would like to come on stage and do their thing for open mic. The twins immediately look at Natosha.

"No" Natosha frowns with a slight smile.

"Come on Tosha, just do a little something." Rosalind begs.

"She is real good." Roxanne tells the guys.   After two people go on, the MC says they have time for one more. The twins get loud to get his attention. The MC then calls Natosha up.

"I am going to get y'all for this." Natosha says as she gets up.

Natosha approaches the microphone as the band softly plays, 'Don't say goodnight' by The Isley Brothers'. As she speaks she takes the crowd by storm. She goes on an intellectual rant of her take on love as she hints at pain. Frank is absolutely blown away, because not only is she beautiful and fine…

This chick's got a head on her shoulders

She concludes her piece with a subliminal message to Frank that he indeed gets as she ends with "I don't want to say goodnight, tonight." The crowd applauds as Natosha comes off stage.

"That was beautiful." Frank says.

"I told you she was nice." Rosalind says.

"Thanks." Notosha says.

The band comes back on for another round of songs. They talk as Frank notices Natosha checking the time on her watch. She explains to them that she needs to catch a cab home so she can get some rest for her brother's wedding. Frank offers to take her home.

"What about your cousin?" Natosha asks.

"Oh girl yall go ahead. We'll get him home safely." Roxanne winks.

Frank walks Natosha to his SUV. He opens the door for her before he gets in. She gives him directions along the way. Frank goes on about how he had such a great time with her. While he talks, Natosha's conscience is having an epic battle in her mind. She thinks about how this guy has been treating her like a lady all night long versus her off and on abusive boyfriend whom hasn't touched her in months.

Hello

They carefully walk to the front door as neither wants to be the one to say goodnight. Frank places his hands on Natosha's hips and looks in her eyes.

"Thanks for such a lovely night." He says.

"Thank **you**." she says as Frank places his hands on her hips, pulling her closer. Natosha runs her hands up his forearms onto his manly biceps then rest them on his shoulders. They stare deeply into each other's eyes as Frank plants an intensifying kiss that triggers her arousal. Natosha lustfully moans as she feels Frank stiffen while pressed against her. After she is completely turned on and can no longer stand it, Natosha invites Frank inside.

On her bed Frank lies back as she straddles him. Natosha grinds her hips slowly in a circular motion, as she lusts him more and more. Summer's heat takes its toll, as the sweat rolls down her bobbling breast. "Oh Frank!" She grinds faster and faster, getting more intense as Natosha sinks her fingernails into Frank's big chest. Natosha's heart races with excitement as she releases a secretion of pleasure. After a few rounds of intense love making, they fall fast asleep.

The morning comes around, Frank awaken by a kiss on the cheek.

"Hey you" she smiles. "Come on, I want to show you something." She gets out of bed and heads towards the door. Frank is hypnotized by her curves she's flaunting in her tank top and boy shorts. (Not to mention that walk.)

"I could wake up to that every morning." Frank mumbles as she stops at the door and looks back at him.

"Come on before you miss it." she implies.

Frank washes up and joins Natosha on the patio for some beignets and coffee.

This **is** beautiful." Frank says.

"When I was growing up here, mornings were always my favorite." Natosha says as they watch the sunrise over the lake just past the back yard, a perfect ending to a beautiful night.

"I see why. It's so peaceful with the birds chirping and all... Is that an alligator over there?"

Oh yeah, that's just Harry, he won't bite." she says as Frank looks at her with an Ice Cube like frown.

"I'm just playing" she laughs. After a while of talking Natosha walks Frank to his SUV.

"So am I going to get to see you again before I leave town?" he asks.

"I'm not sure, I mean, with my brother's big wedding and all."

"If not today, I'd love to come back down here and see you sometime, if it's cool." he says while caressing her hands.

"As much as I'd like that Frank, I just don't want to do the distant relationship thing. Maybe we should let last night be what it was…beautiful."

"Yeah, maybe you're right, even though, Atlanta's not too far from here."

Wait, Did he just say…..

Atlanta, I thought you guys were from Memphis?" A very stunned Natosha asks.

No, Sean's from Memphis, I'm from Atlanta. I couldn't get a word in last night because your friend and he were doing all the talking." he laughs then says to her. "Natosha, I think you're a special person

They say goodbye as Notosha begins to think what rotten luck she has. This is why she hates to take chances. As much as she liked everything about Frank, she felt as if it wasn't completely over with her and Mike.

After some time off and an eventful weekend in New Orleans, Frank returned home. He thought about Natosha from time to time and that night in which they shared. A few months went by into the beginning of fall and everything was back to normal or though it seemed. One particular night at the beginning of shift Frank and Alexis made their routine stop for coffee. Alexis met up with some friends in the store and started talking. Frank got his black coffee and flirted with the cashier, Cynthia, as usual. Alexis walks up to the register with her friends while Frank is carrying on with the cashier.

"Guys, this is my partner Frank Battle." Alexis begins to introduce everyone. Frank turns around and sees that one of her friends is none other than Natosha. Their eyes meet as they are introduced, trying hard not to give away what happened between them.

"Frank, this is my girl Tosha, she's a nurse over at the hospital and this is her fiancé Mike." They all shake hands as Frank holds his composure, but is absolutely blown away on the inside. They talk for a few minutes, then Frank and Alexis begin to patrol the city. Frank rides along in silence as he tries to get a grip on what just happened. The more he thought about it the more frustration set in. 'Why did she lie?' He thought to himself.

On his night off from work, Frank and some of the other officers on the force hang out at a local bowling alley. They spend time together as they do once a month enjoying each other's company. They share some laughs over a few games and some pitchers of beer. Togetherness; this is what makes them such a tight-knit group, this why their bond is so tight, this is what makes them know that they have each other's back while on duty.

Frank was in an on-going conversation with the other officers when Alexis, whom is having a girls night out with Natosha, steps in. He totally ignores the fact that Notasha is even around as they talk. With every glance she gives he looks in the other direction, giving her the cold shoulder. As badly as she wants to explain herself, it is not the time or place. Suddenly opportunity presents itself when Frank excuses himself to the restroom. Natosha in turn does the same. "Frank" she says as she catches up with him. "Look I'm sorry I didn't tell you about him, it's not what you think. We weren't-" He cuts her off. "You know what Natosha? If **that** is you real name. I don't even want to hear it. I'm here, constantly thinking about this chick I met in New Orleans. I come to find out that she's from right here in Atlanta and she's engaged. I really thought it was something special about you. You're no different than the rest of them."

The next day Frank pays a visit to his Uncle. As he pulls up, he sees this mysterious young lady leaving his uncle's house. When Frank gets out and questions his uncle about the young lady, his uncle simply responds. "Oh, that's just somebody trying to sale some insurance. So what brings you out this way? I know you ain't coming to watch football with me without bringing beer." The two walk inside. They start to watch the game John notice that Frank is quiet and not his usual talkative self.

"What's wrong? Cat got your tongue."

"Unc, I met this girl… she's perfect."

"But- You looking as if you lost your best friend or something. What's the problem?"

"She lied to me."

"About what? Hell, everybody lies. Did you talk to her and see why, or did you just fly off the handle as usual." Without saying a word John already knew the answer to his question. "Yall young cats don't know shit, want to be players and don't know the game. If she's the woman that you say she is, talk to her and see what's going with her before jumping to conclusions. Boy, pass me bottle in front of you." John pours a shot of brandy into his glass and begins another one of his so many lectures with Frank.

About midways through the next week Frank and Alexis were out on duty. They responded to a domestic disturbance call at a local apartment complex. They arrived on the scene right after fellow officers; Black and Thomas. Other tenants stand outside on this cold night and look. Alexis gets out of the car, she has this strange look on her face as if something's wrong. "Watts, you okay?"

"Oh my god, it's Natosha." She rushes over to check on her friend, meanwhile Frank assist Officer Black on taking her fiancé into custody. Frank conducts an investigation as he talks to Alexis, Officer Thomas and a witness named Jalisa Fields who lives next door. Just as Frank was getting information from Jalisa, Sergeant McCoy arrives on the scene. Alexis was upset about her friend, but holding her composure, as Officer Thomas explains Natosha's status to Frank. "She's suffering from a black eye and a rib injury from him kicking her." "He did what!" Frank says loudly then walks over to Natosha. He squats down next to her as she sits on front step of the apartment complex.

"Hey, we have paramedics on the way. Are you okay?" Frank sympathizes. Without saying a word, Natosha looks at him all teary-eyed. It was like the ultimate look of defeat, a look that took Frank to a distant dark past. After seeing Natosha like this, Frank got so enraged that he walks back over to the squad car where her fiancé was being held and started ranting.

"You like hitting on women!" He roars as fellow officers and Natosha looks on. "That makes you feel like a big man, huh?"

"Battle, what are you doing?" Sergeant McCoy interrupts. You want to swing at somebody!"

"Battle!"

"Swing at me!" Frank yells as Sergeant McCoy gets all in his grill.

"Dammit, Battle, that's enough! You get your ass in that car and you get the hell out of here right now! That's an order!" Both at a standstill not giving any ground, Frank, angrily says "Yes Sir" as he walks away. Frank and Alexis leaves the scene.

After a while of patrolling she finally got him to talk about his outburst. It turns out that when he was little, his mother was involved with an abusive boyfriend and when he looked into Natosha's eyes all he could see was his mother. "So what finally happened, did your mother leave him or what?" Alexis asked. "Once Uncle Mac caught word of it, let's just say we never heard from him again." Frank reminisces with a smile. This is one of the main reasons Frank has always looked up to his uncle, plus the fact that he has always been there like a father. As for the rest of the night it remained relatively quiet for Frank and Alexis while they were out on duty.

Days later as Natosha moved into her new apartment along with the help of Alexis. She vowed that this would be the last time that she'd put herself through this with Mike and that it was really over between them this time. After they get settled they talk for a while about everything from her miscarriage for him to the abuse. Natosha kicks around the idea of moving back home to New Orleans. With a heavy heart and teary eyes Natosha explains, "I gave him everything I had." Alexis sits next to her and says, "It's not your fault Tosha. Some people don't understand how good they have it until it's all gone. But, whatever you decide, you know I'm here for you" she jokingly continues "and apparently Frank is too. Girl, he scared the hell out of me that night." They laugh as Alexis tries to keep her friend in good spirits as she readies herself for the next chapter of her life.

One night while on duty, Frank has to leave work early due to his uncle being hospitalized. He arrives at the hospital and is greeted by his mother in the waiting room. The doctor comes out and informs them that he had suffered a light stroke and is progressing well. Minutes later Natosha comes to take Frank and his mother to the room to see his uncle. Frank elects to stay in the waiting room a few more minutes as he fights back his emotions. All he can think about is how this great man that he has come to idolize his entire life has no wife or children at his side. Natosha comes back to the waiting room to see if Frank is ready. She can see how it was upsetting him, so she talked to him for a minute, letting him know that everything was fine.

Days later, Natosha and Alexis were at the Beauty salon getting their hair done as well as listening to the latest gossip. Alexis' phone sounds off as she checks it and laughs. She explains that it's one of Frank's many silly texts.

"You two are pretty close huh?" Natosha asks.

"We're cool, but it's not like that. Frank is like a brother. We went to the police academy together and have been close ever since." Alexis explains and then invites her to join her and the guys at the sports bar tonight.

Later that same cold night at Scottie Joe's sports bar and grill, Natosha joins Alexis and the guys from the force. They all sit around discuss their busy work week over some drinks. They carry on for some time trading war stories. After receiving a text, Alexis tells Frank that she has to leave on short notice. Frank being Frank jokingly says to her, "That sounds like a booty call, Lexie." "You know what Frank, shut up. You make me sick." she laughs, knowing he's right. Alexis and Natosha prepare to leave, but Frank convinces Natosha to stay a while longer. One by one the guys depart as Frank and Natosha talk. Through conversation they learn that both lives in walking distance of the bar. As they walk home in the cold Frank notices Natosha folding her arms as if her low cut jacket isn't warm enough. He takes his leather coat and puts it on her shoulders.

"Frank, you're gonna freeze."

"We ain't got far to walk." he says as she looks at him then kisses him on the cheek. He walks her to the front door as shades of that night they shared in New Orleans sets in.

"Now this looks awfully familiar." he says.

"What does?"

"We're at your front door, saying goodnight again." he says as it dawns on her as to what he was talking about.

"Well let's take it slow this time." she says as they kiss and say goodnight.

"Hey Frank, call me sometime." she smiles.

"Sure thing"

For the next few weeks Frank and Natosha became great friends. They got to know each other really well through conversations from frequent phone calls. Frank even stopped by the hospital to see her one night when he was working alone. He brought her some lunch and flowers as her fellow nurses; Allie, Sharon and Zerlinda teased her. There was a lot of clarity between them from what happened in the bayou to their current status. A hint of a relationship was starting to develop between the two.

With thoughts of moving back to New Orleans constantly clouding Natosha's head, she pays Frank a surprise visit one cold Saturday afternoon with the intention on telling him. Natosha is greeted by Frank's mother at the door. Natosha enjoys the company of his mother while Frank is outside fixing on his mother's car. The more Ms. Battle and Natosha talk the more they find that they have a lot in common. She sees where Frank gets his funny side from because his mother is an absolute comedian. Ms. Battle even fills Natosha in on Frank's old nickname (Sugar Bear). Frank finished the job and comes inside. Ms. Battle prepares to leave and says goodbye to Natosha.

"Frank's gonna have to bring you around, so we can talk some more."

"Yes ma'am" Natosha says as she over hears Ms. Battle on her way out tell Frank. "I like her, she's sweet." Frank and Natosha talk as he offers to cook her something. She accepts, but once she sees him fumbling around in the kitchen she quickly realizes that he hasn't a clue about what he's doing. Touched by his kind gesture, she politely takes over then puts together some jambalaya. She gives him a little taste.

"Well what do you think, too spicy or not enough?" she asks. He takes a moment to indulge the flavor.

"I think it's perfect, just like you." he says as he takes the spoon out of her hand and places it on the counter and puts his arms around her.

"Aren't you gonna eat?" she asks.

"Yeah, but, I kind of want the main course right now." He says as she smiles. He kisses her neck as she giggles. He looks into her eyes and starts kissing her as all thoughts of her moving back to New Orleans are suspended from her mind momentarily. All she wants this very minute is him, badly. There in the bedroom, Natosha lies on the bed. Frank slowly kisses each old scar as if he was purposely kissing away all the pain in her life. Frank slides inside of Natosha as she moans lustfully. "I want you Tosha." He whispers as he looks her in the eyes and grinds slowly. "Oh

Frank," she moans as he penetrates her harder and faster. The more intense it got, the louder Frank and Natosha's running conversation got. Natosha held on to Frank tightly as she climaxed. Afterwards they spent the evening enjoying each other's company by the fireplace and watching the snow fall.

A few nights later Frank was back at work and for the early part of the night Alexis didn't seem her usual cheerful self, in fact it's as if there's a little tension. Frank takes a few sip of his black coffee.

"What's eating you tonight Watts are you okay?"

"Oh, I'm fine Battle. What's up with you?"

"What do you mean?"

"How're you gonna date my best friend? Frank, she's been through a lot and **you** know how much you love women." she says as they pull over and argue.

"Oh so you're saying I'm not good enough for her."

"Frank your relationships never end well for whomever you date and you know it." They say the truth hurts and no one likes to face that person in the mirror, especially Frank Battle. So he soaks in what Alexis has just said then says tells her something totally unexpected.

You know, I've dated a lot of girls, but I've never felt like this about any of em. The way she converses and the way she carries herself like a lady. I can't stop thinking about her." Frank says, catching Alexis totally off guard. Alexis sees that Frank is being sincere and then drops the bombshell about Natosha spending Thanksgiving in New Orleans and possibly moving back.

Thanksgiving Day has arrived and it's all about good food, family, and friends. While celebrating the holiday, Natosha enjoys time with loved ones, but feels this emptiness inside as if something's missing. "It's gonna be so good having you back at home baby sis. You're the only one with all of Grandma's recipes." Her brother, Terry says as she smiles.

Meanwhile, in Atlanta, Frank is celebrating the holiday as well at his mother's. He is joined by his Uncle John, who keeps on about a surprise, and a cousin from Memphis, Malik Jackson and his wife Angela and children. They are soon joined by this same mysterious young lady which Frank seen leaving his Uncle John's house a while back. His uncle gets everyone's attention and introduces the young lady as his daughter Janelle. Everyone welcomes her to the family. John tells Frank that they were preparing to do a DNA test that day when he saw her leaving from his house.

"Welcome to the family cousin. We're definitely going to do some catching up," Frank says to Janelle. He talks to Malik about his current situation. Then Malik gives him some advice. "Angela and I were in a similar situation. I almost missed out on a great woman. I thank God for everyday we're together. Frank if she means that much to you, tell her." Malik says as Frank takes heed. Frank steps away from the family to get some privacy and to call Natosha. On the other end Natosha excited to hear his voice, does the same to get privacy as well. They talk for a while about the holiday and family. He asks about the rumor of her leaving, she answers honestly and states that nothing's etched in stone just yet and that she just needed time. And just before they say goodbye leaves her with something to think about.

"Natosha, I know you've been through a lot and I definitely understand if you don't want to see anybody right now. But if you do, please consider **us**."

Natosha arrives back at her place, fresh off her trip from New Orleans. Meanwhile Frank was at work, out on patrol with Alexis. Natosha unpacks, takes a shower, and is about to settle in for the night. Frank and Alexis respond to a call on a possible breaking and entering at a local business. Natosha sits down to watch television, she then hears a knock at the door. Frank and Alexis arrive on the crime scene met by Officers Tony Wilson and Marshall Boatwright. Natosha answers the door only to find Mike, her ex-fiancé, paying her a visit. Meanwhile the four officers approach the building as gunshots begin to ring out.

"Everybody get down!!" Officer Boatwright yells as they all shield themselves behind their squad cars. "We got shots fired, we need back up! Repeating we need back up!" Officer Wilson says to dispatch. Frank being Frank chooses not to wait and has another one of his episodes. "Battle, what the hell are you doing?" Alexis asks as Frank scopes out the scene. He explains his plan to go around back and flush the suspect out with teargas. "Watts, you and Boatwright cover the front and Wilson and I'll go round back. This S.O.B. is coming with us tonight." Frank says as Wilson and he make their move. Watts shakes her head and looks at Boatwright as he smiles and says, "That's **your** partner."

Not too far away at Natosha's apartment, Mike uninvitingly makes his way into her apartment. "What are you doing here?" Natosha asks. "Oh I can't come to see my girl?" he asks. "You know what Mike; I fooled myself for a long time when I was with you. I used to convince myself that you would someday somehow change. I actually thought I had something. But you know what, you are tired. You are a tired excuse of a man. I've got somebody that really cares about me now. So you can just take you little tired ass right back out that door you just came in and go find Yolanda. That's right, I know she carrying your baby." He walks back out the door and before he can say something out the way she slams the door in his face. Natosha sits back down then her cell phone goes off. She thinks its Mike and is about ready to go off. But it turns out to be Alexis, texting for her to come to the hospital because Frank had been shot.

All along the way to the hospital Natosha's heart races as her head is over come with all sorts of what ifs. She was so discombobulated that she failed to realize that she left her phone right where she got her text message. When she arrives she runs into a few of his fellow officers. She tunes everyone out that was saying that he was okay until she sees Frank for herself coming out of the emergency room. Natosha rushes right into his arms. Frank sees the concern on her face.

"I'm okay. The bullet just grazed me." Frank says.

"Don't ever do that to me again Frank. I thought I lost you." She says to him as he sees the concern on her face. He puts his arm around her as they walkout the hospital together.

"So does this mean you're not leaving Atlanta?"

"Oh I'm not going anywhere. I'm staying right here with you...Sugar Bear," she says with a smile as Frank looks at her suspiciously.

"Have you been talking to my mom again?" He asks as she smiles. As they are about to say goodbye, Frank looks at her. "I love you Natosha." "I love you too Frank."

Frank walks back to his squad car with Alexis as Sergeant McCoy pulls up. He congratulates him on the arrest. He also tells

Frank that Lieutenant Henderson had a few choice words for him and would like to see him in her office along with Captain Gibson. See a few years ago when Frank was just a rookie on the force Captain Gibson was his Lieutenant. She stayed on his case even more so than his current Lieutenant.

Over the course of the next few months Frank and Natosha began seeing each other heavily. One evening as Natosha was driving she was pulled over by a squad car. Officer Wilson got out of the car.

"Hey how are you doing ma'am. I need to see your license and registration please."

"Is there a problem officer?" Natosha says. She then recognizes Officer Wilson. "Hey Tony, what's going on? It's me Tosha."

"You're Lexie's friend right. I remember you. Yeah we got a call on a suspicious vehicle like yours. I'm sure everything is o.k. but I just need to run your license any way." Officer Wilson says as he walks to his car. A few minutes two more squad cars pull up. Officer Wilson comes back with a bit of bad news.

"Hey Tosha, I don't know exactly what's going on, but I'm going to need you to come with me."

"What! This must be some kind of mistake." Natosha says as her heart races. They walk to the car as Frank gets out of the back of Officer Wilson's car with a ring box. Frank gets down on one knee as the tears of joy stream down Natosha's face as he proposes to her. She immediately says yes. His fellow officers including Alexis stand around clapping and cheering.

After months of planning and preparing, they got married that summer. Soon afterwards, Natosha gave birth to a baby girl. After seeing his little girl, Frank began to see things differently.

He took better care of himself on the job and was no longer the loose cannon he once was. He was promoted to the sergeant's position. Frank and Natosha reached the highest point of happiness. Once a year they visit New Orleans as a reminder of how they met that hot summer's day down in the bayou.

· · · · ·

The Fielder's Choice

As the crisp winds of fall blow in, the season is nearly over for the boys of summer. For pro baseball player Aaron Henry it only means playoff time. Aaron is one of the game's premier third basemen for New York. During his career he took to the spotlight with ease. Aaron landed lots of endorsements with shoe companies and food chains, he even guest appeared on numerous of talk shows. Aaron was on his way to winning a second pennant in four years with New York. Aaron and his teammates were in a three games to one lead in a best of seven championship series against Washington DC.

On a night before game five in Washington, Aaron was at a restaurant where he ran into an old friend from his neighborhood named Nakitia Davison. Nakitia is now a politician in DC whom is looking to run for congress in a year. The two decide to go to her place to do some catching up and get away from the public's eye as well.

The following night, in game five, New York went on to win the championship series in Washington. Like so many times before, Aaron gave his all. He fell just short of being named the series MVP, but to him it didn't matter. At the end of the day, his team was once again champions.

One year later, after a prolific Hall of Fame career in New York, Aaron was traded to Miami. Aaron injured his knee in an exhibition game with his new team. The fact that Aaron is now thirty-seven and in the twilight of his career some feel his career maybe over sooner than later. He suffers with the aches and pains of anyone else his age in sports. He may not heal as quickly as he used to, but with the strong upbringings he endured in Altonville Alabama as a child, Aaron has too much fight in him to quit. After a minor surgery Aaron's injury required a few weeks of therapy. Aaron contacted one of the area's best to work with on his therapy.

A few days later Aaron was set to begin therapy. He got a knock at the door and was greeted by a very beautiful Puerto Rican lady named Tatiana Perez. Tatiana is just as beautiful on the inside with a great sense of humor. She is also a very supportive mother to her fifteen-year-old athletic daughter Jasmine. She comes in and introduces herself. They then talk business and get acquainted. She takes a look at Aaron's knee and gets right to work on some simple exercises. Being that Tatiana works with pro ball players all the time, she is not star struck by Aaron even though she is very aware of who he is. During therapy Aaron is his normal talkative self. He talks to her about the game, his injury, and how his agent often tries to get him to promote himself at times for publicity. He explains to her about a star studded benefit dinner he's attending in which his agent has set up a date with a hot super model.

Aaron is rich and famous, he is very humble and doesn't like to be labeled or placed in that class. Aaron never forgot where he came from. He grew up without a whole lot and throughout his pro career his close friends from home always kept him well grounded. Unsure if he wanted to take part in the event, he asks Tatiana for her opinion as they take a break.

"It'll probably be fun." she says.

"I just don't like being around a bunch of snobs ya know."

"Well, just be yourself and not who they want you to be." she simply says.

"Maybe I should take you instead. I mean, being that you aren't married are anything."

"No I'm not married and for the record, I don't date athletes." she politely says to him.

"Oh what's wrong dating athletes?"

"You guys are always on the road in major cities doing God knows what with women who constantly throw themselves at you just to get money for an illegitimate child that you won't take care of."

So you got me all figured out huh. Well, I'd hate to disappoint you but I'm at a point in my career where I'm pretty much of a homebody who just happens to be childless." He says to an impressed Tatiana.

"Like I said, I don't date athletes. Besides, I'm too old for you anyways."

"I'm 37 which is considered old in sports. I know better than to ask a woman her age, so I'm guessing you're 33 or 34 tops, whatever it is it looks good on you." Aaron says as Tatiana smiles and takes it as a compliment. They then get back to work.

On the night of the star studded benefit dinner, Aaron was in attendance with his super model date as she stopped, smiled and posed for every camera in the place. She even took the liberty of teasing the media answering questions of the two being an item. Once it was over Aaron only bided her farewell and skipped the after party.

Aaron got back to therapy the following week. He was once again talkative, whereas Tatiana was relatively quiet as if she had something on her mind. "You okay?" Aaron asked. She explained that she had been selected to coach her daughter's summer league softball team and had the slightest idea of how to coach the girls. Aaron offered to help since he was still on the injured list. Tatiana was unsure at first but realizing that she could use the help. She eventually took him up on his offer.

their first day of practice Aaron showed up and talked to the girls. The girls didn't really recognize Aaron, being that none of them were baseball fanatics; all they knew was that Jasmine's mom had a fine boyfriend. He then gave them pointers on the basics throwing, catching and hitting. He positioned them all according to their strengths and weaknesses. He placed Jasmine on second base. He then hit the ball to them and discussed certain situations and where to throw the ball. Aaron broke down the game to the girls and defined all of the details to them, removing all self-doubt as an impressed Tatiana watched.

For the next two weeks Aaron continued therapy and helping Tatiana with the girls. He continued to flirt with her at times during therapy. And though she didn't show it, but the more she got to know him, she kind of had a thing for him. In a sense, he was growing on her. The thing that was drawing Tatiana to Aaron was how down-to-earth he seemed for a person of his stature. There was no arrogance about him at all, not mention the fact that there seemed to be a good connection between him and Jasmine as well. Once Aaron's knee started to strengthen up he got back on weights. One day at the gym after he'd finished strength training, he ran into Tatiana. Aaron couldn't help but notice how nice Tatiana was looking in her spandex. She told him that she was on her way to cardio class. As usual Aaron would talk and tease then flirt with Tatiana.

"So when are you going to let me take you out?" Aaron asked her.

"Tell you what; if you can hang with me for an hour in my cardio class, I'll let you take me out." Tatiana says as she smiles.

"Piece of cake" Aaron confidently says as he takes her up on the wager. They walk into the studio together as she introduced him.

"Hey ladies this is Aaron, he's going to join us today. Aaron, this is Janet, Doreen, Teresa, Jo, Shay, Debbie, Yvonne and this is our fearless leader Maria." Tatiana says.

They started off with some warm up exercises as Aaron, still cocky, winks his eye at Tatiana. After the warm up, then came all the real exercises. It was like fifty minutes of hell in that class. Tatiana laughed as Aaron kept giving off a look like 'are you serious'. Afterwards Tatiana asked Aaron where he was going to take her. "I'll be lucky if I can walk tonight. I think she tried to kill me." Aaron said as he grunts. "Aww, poor baby" Tatiana teases.

That night Aaron and Tatiana went to see a movie and after that they walked on the beach. They got to know each other personally as they sat down and talked. Tatiana explained that Jasmine's father was killed in a drug deal gone wrong when she was very young.

"You're the only male friend I've had that's made an effort to reach out to her. She seems to like you."

Oh I love kids." Aaron said as he explained that he was once engaged to marry but soon broke it off. He then explained why.

I'm infertile, I can't have kids. I didn't want her to suffer because of my condition nor was I willing to adopt." He says as Tatiana shows concern.

"Aaron, you can correct this through medical treatments." She says.

"Yeah, but after you've seen a few specialist you start to lose hope." Aaron says as Tatiana looks at him and takes him by the hand and lays her head on his shoulder. They enjoy the calm breeze as they watch the waves roll onto shore. Aaron starts to run his fingers through Tatiana's long black curly hair.

"Aaron, this city is filled with lots of young beautiful women. I'm forty-three, what's so special about me?"

You're a very beautiful woman and I like being around you. It's just something about you that reminds me of home." He says to her as she gives off a huge smile. Aaron then places his hand on her cheek and gives her long passionate kiss. They then walk back up the beach to his vehicle. Along the way home Tatiana tells him she's coming down with a headache. Aaron offers to stop and get aspirins, but she explains that she's allergic to aspirins. He takes her home and walks her to the door. She thanks him for such a nice evening.

"Now are you sure you don't want me to come in and watch over you through the night? Cause you know I would." Aaron says being silly.

"I'll bet you would." Tatiana says as he then kisses her goodnight. She goes inside and sees Jasmine and some of her friends are still up watching movies. She walks through and the girls start to tease her about her date with Aaron as she smiles. "Go to bed girls" Tatiana says as she goes up stairs and gets ready for bed herself.

Tatiana lies down in bed. As she gets up in the middle of the night, she looks next to her and sees Aaron lying next to her. He places his finger on her lip before she could say a word. He started kissing her lips then on the neck and breast. She couldn't seem to tear herself away from him nor did she want to as he lay on top of her. She moaned and squeezed him tightly as he grinded her. She exhales as she climaxes and then opens her eyes and realizes that it was only a dream. She sits up in her bed and sees that it is 1:00 am in the morning as she tries to make sense of this dream.

following Monday Aaron was at his final day of therapy. Tatiana came by as they went right to work exercising. During what was their final session, Tatiana kept having visions of her dream about Aaron. She remained professional as she worked out with him, though occasionally she'd catch a glimpse of his appealing physique and wonder. Afterwards they talked for a little while. Aaron thanked her for everything and gave her a gift basket of goodies as an extra. They were about to say goodbye. "I'll be playing minor league ball in a couple of weeks, working my way back up to the majors. I know you don't date athletes, but I'd love it if I could see you again sometime." Aaron says to her. Tatiana then invites Aaron to the girls' last game coming up Saturday.

When Saturday arrived the girls were losing early in the game, but came back for a triumphant win. To celebrate their victory, Aaron invited Tatiana and the girls over for a pool party and some barbecue. Aaron and Tatiana chaperoned for the girls while they had fun swimming. Later on Jasmine asked Tatiana if she could go with some of the girls to a party. Tatiana didn't want her to go, but Aaron spoke up for Jasmine.

"Aw, give her a little space, she's a teen now. Let her have a little fun." Aaron says to Tatiana.

"Easy for you to say, you don't have any kids to worry about." Tatiana says without thinking and then it dawns on her about Aaron's condition. She quickly apologizes as Aaron understands that it wasn't said blatantly. After a little more convincing from Aaron, Tatiana decides to let Jasmine go along with the girls. Tatiana gave her a curfew as Jasmine thanks her mom. "Thanks Mr. Henry, you're the bomb." Jasmine says to Aaron being that he talked Tatiana into letting her go with her friends. With clinched fists, Aaron and Jasmine, bump knuckles as Tatiana looks with a smirk.

After the girls left, Aaron and Tatiana cleaned up then decided to get in the pool for a swim. Tatiana took off her waist wrap revealing her nice derriere as Aaron stood in admiration. "Are you sure you're forty-three? Because your body looks like it stopped at thirty and lost track of time." Aaron says as Tatiana smiles. "Hey, eyes up here." Tatiana jokingly says, pointing at her face as she notices Aaron checking her out. They get into the pool and go for a swim. After a while they stop and talk as they sit on the edge of the pool with their feet still in the water.

"So Aaron, how did you get into baseball?"

"I was about seven when my best friend's dad used to round up some of us kids from the neighborhood and teach us how to play the game of baseball. I was pretty good at it, so he signed me up and made sure I stuck with it. Even when I wanted to quit he wouldn't let me. He saw something in me and was always there for me. I guess that's why I've always considered him as my dad." Aaron says as he reminisces.

"What about your real dad, if you don't mind me asking?" Tatiana says.

"He walked out on us before I was born. He turned up a few years after I made it in the pros, only to ask for money." Aaron recalls those hurtful memories of his mother struggling to make ends meet for his sister and him.

"Wow…That's some story Aaron." Tatiana says with empathy as she places her hand on his. "For the record, I think you turned out fine." She then kisses him on the cheek as they talk a little while longer.

"Well, I should be going. There's no telling what time Jasmine's coming home." she says.

"Tatiana, it's still early. She'll be fine." he says as they get out of the pool. "You just stay here and keep me company." he says with a devilish grin.

"Why?" she asks as he places his hands at her waist.

"Because I want you to." he says as they engage in a kiss. Aaron and Tatiana leave the pool then get into a hot shower together. They lather up as the water rinses the suds down their bodies. They interlock in a deep kiss. Tatiana holds this stud of a man close as he gently caresses and kisses her breast. She leans back against the wall of the shower as Aaron lifts her leg and enters her slowly. They start making love as Aaron grunts and Tatiana lustfully moans. Things got more intense in the shower as they start to grind harder. Tatiana moans and speaks whinny in Spanish as she calls Aaron papi. He holds her tight while climaxing. Afterwards they talk as they enjoy the scenery and each other's company from the balcony of his bedroom.

The weekend before Aaron has to report to his minor league team he makes a stop in his hometown. He gives his mom and big sister (Aaliyah) a surprise visit. After seeing his mother and sister, Aaron goes next door to see an older couple (Mr. and Mrs. Daniels) who had helped make him into the man he had become. When Aaron was growing up his mother struggled to make ends meet and didn't have a lot. Whenever they needed food or money for bills Mr. and Mrs. Daniels was right there and Aaron was forever grateful to this day. As Aaron leaves the Daniels home he runs into another neighbor on the sidewalk named Mrs. Bethel Davison walking with her one-year-old grandson. Aaron stops gives her a hug and talks for a minute.

"How've you been Mrs. Davison?"

"I'm doing fair son. You done got so big, I liked to not recognized ya. How you been doing child?"

"I'm fine. Is this one of your grandbabies?"

"Yeah, with his **bad** behind" Mrs. Davison says as she holds a switch in her other hand as she continues. "Yeah this is Nikitia's baby."

"I didn't know Nakitia had kids."

"Oh she just got one. You know she's running for office up there in Washington so I'm taking care of him for right now until she gets situated." Mrs. Davison says. They then bid each other farewell.

Aaron drives around the block to see his best friend Eric Daniels. Aaron walks around to the back where he sees his best friend Eric and his sons working on this old car. Eric has back turned. Aaron puts his index finger to his lips, telling the boys not to say anything.

"Hey man do you know what you're doing under that hood." Aaron says as Eric turns around. They embrace each other and laugh.

"What are you doing here?" Eric says all filled with excitement. Aaron explains that he's in town for one night. He explains that his knee is healthy. Aaron also tells Eric about his new girlfriend whom he was going to bring home once the season was over. He then tells Eric that he'd just came from his parent's house as they start reminiscing.

"Man you remember when your daddy took me, you, Travis and Jamaal and beat our ass for smoking and setting his shed on fire?" Aaron laughs.

"Hell yeah, your bad ass got me in a lot of shit."

"I just couldn't figure out why you wouldn't tell on me when I did stuff." Aaron says.

I felt so bad for you when dad used to whip you. I always looked at you as my little brother and I knew daddy was going to whip me harder than you." Eric says with all seriousness. This is the bond between the two of them. This is why they refer to each other as brother. Aaron talked about possibly coming back home after he retires to coach high school baseball. Later they were joined by Jamaal and Travis as they talked about old times until it was dark.

Aaron went on to play minor league ball for a few games and then he made his return to the majors. He played the game without missing a beat. He was even a fan favorite and voted to play in the All-Star game. While Aaron was off playing ball he called

Tatiana every chance he got. Things were starting to blossom for the two of them.

Aaron was back in Miami when Tatiana hosted a backyard barbecue to celebrate Jasmine's sixteenth birthday. He came by for a visit. He was greeted by Jasmine and some of the girls from softball. Tatiana was sitting next to her sister, Nichelle Perez, whom was in town from Washington D.C.

So that's Aaron huh" Nichelle asked Tatiana.

"Yep" Tatiana smiles.

"You did good Chicka. So how is he?"

"**Blessed**" Tatiana says in admiration as Nichelle is stunned at her response.

"Oh my god Helena, I can't believe you just said that. I meant, how is he as a person, silly?" Nichelle says (calling Tatiana by her first name) as they laugh. Aaron comes over and gives Tatiana a hug and kiss. He then met Tatiana's friends and her sister Nichelle.

While at Jasmine's party Aaron fitted in well with Tatiana's friends as he sat next to her. Nichelle drilled Aaron about the dos and don'ts of dating her big sister. She began to demonstrate what would happen to him if he mistreated Tatiana. She shook her fist at him speaking Spanish; Aaron held his hands up as if he were surrendering as they all laughed. Aaron also did a little bonding with Jasmine during the party. He explained to Jasmine how much he cared for Tatiana and her and how he wanted to be a part of their lives. Jasmine was fond of the idea, knowing how happy he made her mother.

After the season was over Aaron got to spend a little more time with Tatiana. Jasmine was now in her final year of high school and an honor student. Aaron hinted at the idea of Jasmine going to college at his Alma mater in Atlanta. With Aaron and Tatiana becoming more serious in their relationship he felt like the time was right to introduce Tatiana to his family at home in Altonville.

It was Homecoming weekend in Altonville and Aaron came home for his twenty-year class reunion. On a Friday morning Aaron, Tatiana and Jasmine settled in at his mother's home. They got acquainted with his mom and his sister who'd taken the day off from work. During the day Aaron attended festivities with high school classmates. He took her to his old high school where he plans to come back and coach baseball once he retires. That evening they enjoyed watching his home team crush the opposing team 38-0. Not to mention his best friend Eric Daniels was at the helm in his inaugural season as head coach.

After the game Jasmine met Eric's twin sons then joined them at the homecoming dance. Tatiana joined Aaron and his classmates at a reunion party. Aaron was so overwhelmed seeing everyone together again. Aaron introduced Tatiana to his friends as they all swapped old stories. Also in attendance were fellow classmates Nakitia Davison and her cousin Renee. Nakitia is now in the political field and doing well, whereas Renee is still the same drama queen she was in high school. Renee once had a thing for Aaron back in school as she did for every other guy that was popular. Her big mouth and bad attitude turned most guys away including Aaron. Now with the fact of what conspired between Aaron and Nikitia, Renee feels empowered by her envious ambitions.

"There's Mr. Baseball. You need to go on over there and talk to him Nikki." Renee says.

"Renee, you need to chill out okay." Nakitia says as she walks over to the refreshment table. While Nakitia was getting some refreshments, Aaron walked up.

"Hi Aaron" She says as he walks up.

"Nikki, hey girl how you doing" Aaron says excitingly as they embrace each other. They talk for a minute or two. "Aaron, can I have a word-" She was quickly cut off by Tatiana and another classmate walking up. Aaron introduced Nikitia to his girlfriend Tatiana as one of the guys mentioned how much Nikitia stays in the public eye. "Man, every time you look around Nikki is on TV." While they all talked, someone started to crank the party up a notch by talking loudly on the microphone. It was none other than Eric whom was out and about celebrating his teams win. Eric was accompanied by an old friend and new assistant principal, Lanita Fields.

The next day Aaron, Tatiana, Eric and Lanita all went to the fall fest while Jasmine went to the fair with Eric's sons. Aaron and Eric clowned around with the girls a bit as they felt like teens on a double date. Later that evening the four of them sat at Eric's place having some drinks as Tatiana listened to old stories about growing up in Altonville. She listened to stories of how bad Aaron was when they were little. Tatiana absolutely loved the atmosphere of this small town and its people.

Weeks later in Miami, three of Aaron's closest friends in the game were in town. They got together at Aaron's to watch the final game of the World Series. Fellow ball players; Chris Jones, Dan Creech and Mike West came by to pay Aaron a visit. As it turns out the guys were actually trying to recruit Aaron to come play with them in Atlanta.

"Come on man. I know you still got a little gas left in the tank." Dan says.

"And Miami's not going anywhere any time soon. We're trying to make the playoffs, this coming season. We need you." Chris interrupts.

"Yeah, but I'm still under contract with Miami." Aaron says.

"That's why we're here. The front office is going to take care of everything. All we need is a yes from you and they'll do the rest to have you traded to Atlanta." Mike says. Aaron then puts it into consideration as he wonders about the effect it would have on his relationship with Tatiana.

In early December Aaron and a few friends got together for an evening cruise aboard a yacht. It was also Tatiana's birthday. The scenery was beautiful that evening as the yacht cruised just off the coast. They were red-carpet ready. Aaron looked dapper in his black tuxedo. Tatiana looked elegant in her red evening gown with the split up the leg and open toe stilettoes. He finally broke the news to her about the possibility of playing for Atlanta and having her join him. Tatiana was skeptical of the idea of moving to another city with Aaron.

"Aaron, I don't know, I mean, we're not even married?" Tatiana insisted.

"Yeah, you're right." Aaron says as he nods at the waiter. "But what if we were?" Aaron smiles as the waiter walks up beside Tatiana with a silver platter. He lifts the dome from the platter and there was a beautiful diamond ring. Tatiana's face lit up with the biggest smile. He proposed as his friends cheered him on. She was flattered and immediately said yes. Out on the deck they slow danced as the band played. Tatiana rested her head on Aaron's chest as they danced; wishing this moment could last forever.

As their date came to an end, Aaron took her home. He walked her to the door he saw her again admiring her ring and smiling.

"You like it?" he asks.

"It's okay" she says being silly.

"Okay?" he says aloud as they laugh.

"I'm kidding Aaron, I love it." Tatiana says.

"I love you" he says and starts kissing her passionately. Aaron runs his hands down Tatiana waist. She holds him tighter as she kisses him harder. She eventually opens the door as they go upstairs. In her bedroom she continues kissing him softly while unbuttoning his tux. Aaron undoes her gown as she lies back on her bed. He caresses and kisses her breast. Tatiana sighs as he enters between her thighs and grind slowly. "Oh Aaron" Tatiana whiningly moans as Aaron continuously grinds her deeper and harder. The repetition of thrust of his shaft inside of her intensified her desire for him. Aaron grinds faster as Tatiana holds tightly as she climaxes with him.   About a week later Aaron and Tatiana were back in Altonville. They were invited and attended Altonville's annual Christmas Ball while in town. Aaron and Tatiana sat at their table dressed to the tee. One by one more and more people showed up for the ball. This year's Honoree was none other than Altonville's own Nikitia Davison. She gave a brief welcome speech to everyone and then it was on to the festivities.

Nikitia was enjoying the evening with her new boyfriend. Nikitia's cousin Renee was around as well. Renee was well into having her share of drinks and having something negative to say about everyone at the ball.

There's one in every family
Renee, you need to slow down alright."

"Aw Nikki, I'm just having little fun girl" Renee says as Nikitia rolls her eyes and walks away from her. Moments later, Renee runs into Tatiana and sees her huge engagement ring. A few drinks later Renee approaches Aaron when Tatiana walks to the restroom. She talks to him at first and then she tries to get all up on him. "Girl, what the hell's wrong with you?" Aaron says as he steps back. Nikitia, who'd been watching Renee, walks up and try to prevent a commotion while people began to watch. Nikitia grabs Renee by the arm. "Come on. You're drunk, you need to go home and quit embarrassing yourself." Nikitia says as Renee jerks her arm away. "Oh I'm the embarrassment? I'm just being me. I ain't got shit to hide unlike you Senator." She says out loud as Nikitia gives off this evil look. "You need to tell Aaron about his son!" Renee blurts out in her drunken anger. Aaron looks at Nikitia then looks over at Tatiana whom had just walked back over. Nikitia immediately snaps and lunges over and was about to slap Renee as the crowd breaks it up. Renee was then escorted out. "What is she talking about Nikki?" Aaron asks. Nikitia then walks out of the ball too upset to explain.

Tatiana had little understanding about the situation. She felt like Aaron was a liar and could not be trusted. He tried to plead with her, but she wasn't having it. On that long flight to Miami, the tension was so thick it could've been cut with a knife. As a result in this, Tatiana gave his ring back and called off all plans for a wedding. While this was going on, the time was up for Aaron to make his decision on a trade. With their relationship now on ice and no return calls, Aaron chose to go play in Atlanta.

On a random night Aaron got an anonymous phone call. To his surprise it was Nakitia calling. She finally came around to tell him the truth about their one night stand that led to their son. She apologized as she explained that her candidacy in politics was the reasoning behind her secrecy.

"With you being a famous ball player and me a politician, the media would love nothing more than to air our dirty laundry." she says.

So what's his name?" Aaron asked her.

"Jaquan" she says as Aaron was in awe.

"Wow, not everyone knows my middle name."

"Yeah, well I'm not everyone. I'm the same little girl you used to hide in the bushes and throw rocks at when I rode my bike, until that day Eric's dad caught you." she says as they laugh and reminisce. Nikitia then explains that she and boyfriend don't intend on breaking up, but working on their relationship.

Nikitia was already certain of Aaron being the father, she had a DNA test done with him. After it proved to be 99.999, Aaron became the best father his son could ask for. Almost all of his free time was spent with his son. He became to his son the father that he never had. And now with his new found joy of becoming a father Aaron still felt that certain emptiness without Tatiana. Though friends tried to set him up on dates occasionally, he really missed Tatiana. In desperation he left her one last message on her voice mail.

Meanwhile back in Miami, Tatiana continued doing therapy with injured ball players. Her sister Nichelle was in town as they went out on a Friday night. They were at a local club just having a few drinks and talking.

"So how are things between you and Aaron?"

There is no me and Aaron. It's over." Tatiana says as she takes a sip of her martini

"Helena, didn't you say that all of that took place before you met him. Don't you think that you're being a little selfish Chicka?" Nichelle says.

"No" Tatiana responds with an ice cold look.

Well, what does your heart say? I saw how happy you were with him. Helena now is not the time to be proud. Don't let a good thing pass you by. That's all I'm saying." Nichelle says as they continue to talk and enjoy their night out. Though Tatiana gave the impression that she didn't miss Aaron, deep inside she did as she took heed to what Nichelle had just said.

Aaron, now the new face in Atlanta, is in what is to be his final season playing professional baseball. One day during spring training with his new teammates, Aaron was interrupted. One of the staff members came to Aaron. "Hey, Mr. Henry, There are some young ladies here to see you. They said that they are your daughters." Aaron walked inside all puzzled. In the hall he was met by Jasmine and a couple of the girls he coached.

"Hey what are you guys doing all the way up here in Atlanta?" he asks.

"We came to tour the University and do some site-seeing on our spring break and since we were in Atlanta we decided to come by and surprise you." Jasmine says to Aaron.

"Oh okay. So how'd you guys find the training facility?" he asks.

Some policeman named Officer Battle or something led us here."

"Cool, so how's your mom?" Aaron asks Jasmine.

"Why don't you ask **her?**" Jasmine says as her and the girls giggle. Aaron turns around and sees Tatiana. "Hey you" Tatiana says. He then gives her the biggest hug, lifting her off of the ground. "I have missed you so much." he says as he puts her back down. "I missed you too Aaron."   With Tatiana and the girls being in town for a few of days, it gave her and Aaron time to patch things up. The girls were chauffeured around Atlanta shopping. Tatiana and Aaron got to spend time together at his upscale apartment down town. Over a glass of wine and conversation, they enjoyed the nice view of the city. They talked for a while and did some catching up with each other. Tatiana then sets her pride aside and tries to break the ice.

"Aaron, I…" she sighs as she struggles to find the words to apologize for breaking up with him. Aaron sits next to her and places her hands into his.

"Hey, it's okay. The important thing is that you're here…I understand why you did what you did. You had every right to be upset with me. I can't have kids, but yet I have a son. Tatiana, I'm sorry I hurt you, but understand I make no apologies for my son." He says as she nods her head.

"So, how is he?" Tatiana asks.

"**Bad**, I don't know where he gets it from." Aaron says. Being that she's heard a lot about his mischievous childhood, Tatiana gives him the look as they laugh. Aaron then convinces Tatiana to give their relationship another try. He assures her that there wouldn't be any more surprises, she then accepts.

In the spring Jasmine graduated from high school and immediately began college at the University in Atlanta. Tatiana moved to Atlanta as well to be with her now on again fiancé Aaron. Tatiana became an awesome step-mother to Aaron's son; as he stole her heart from the get go. Aaron and his team went through a great season. He was named comeback athlete of the year. His team fell just short of going to the championship series. After the season Aaron retired from baseball with honors and a high hopeful to be inducted into the hall of fame.

Aaron and Tatiana married and spent their honeymoon in Puerto Rico. They moved into a new home in Altonville where he returned to his old high school as the baseball team's new manager. Tatiana began working as a therapist at the town's hospital where they lived together happily.

· · · · ·

In The Game Of X's and O's

The year was 1987, eighties rock had all but run it's coarse. Hip hop was in its purest form and on the verge of evolution. And a torch was being passed from Luther Vandross to Keith Sweat as R&B's balladeer. And in a small town in the southern parts of Alabama called Altonville, life was good in junior high for eighth grader Eric Daniels. On a Sunday afternoon Eric was at park with older sister Teresa, but soon ventured off with friends, Travis Davis, Jamaal Dawson and Aaron Henry. While in the park, they watched some of the older guys from their neighborhood rapping along with a DJ. Eric had big aspirations to rap some day and was taking it all in as the guys were doing their thing. Eric was so caught up in the moment that he failed to notice Jalisa Fields, his friend from school, walk up next to him. She speaks to the guys and tells Eric that Teresa was looking for him.

Eric walked with Jalisa through the park as she pointed out his sister. It was a moment Eric would remember for a long time to come. Eric looked across the park and it was as if time had stood still. In a word Eric was flabbergasted by this pretty girl talking to his sister.

"Who is that in the flowered shorts?" Eric asks Jalisa

Oh that's my sister Nita and the other girl is our friend Marissa. Why, you want to talk to her?" Jalisa teases with him. Eric walks over and Teresa introduces them all. They then leave the park before it gets dark. Along the ride home and later that night, all Eric could think about was Jalisa's sweet sister Lanita.

He thought so much about her that he even wrote a rap song about her while in class. The only problem is that he sat in the back, right next to Jalisa. So when he was excused to go to the restroom, Jalisa just happened to look over at his tablet and see her sister's name. Needless to say she read his song about her big sister and was flattered. Being that they go way back to the fifth grade, he didn't get upset with her for reading it; he only asked that she'd not tell her sister. Jalisa blackmailed Eric about it a few times. She promised that she wouldn't mention it, though eventually she did.

As summer came around, Eric and the guys played baseball in the city league when they weren't at the park swimming or just hanging out. One of their favorite spots to go during summer was the Skating Rink, local hot spot for all the teens and tweens. For fourteen year olds; Eric, Travis and Jamaal it was the place to be. Though Aaron was two years younger, he was never far behind especially with the fact he stayed next door to Eric. In some ways Eric was like a big brother to Aaron.

eating junk food and playing some video games the guys were checking out the girls. Eric was the oldest, but always the shyest of the guys. So it was no surprise when Travis and Jamaal got out on the dance floor, being that they were more outgoing.

Aaron had just beaten Eric in a video game when Eric looked across a crowded room and saw Lanita coming in along with Jalisa and Marissa. Eric was completely in a daze, longing to be the one to some way, somehow sweep Lanita off her feet. Just the thought of this cute petite girl with the big gold hoop ear rings shining through her neck length Jheri curl. Her quiet and shy-like ways and nice smile were an absolute turn on for Eric. Each time he'd get the chance to talk to her; he'd stumble over words as if his tongue had two left feet, his palms got sweaty and sometimes he'd just speak and walk away. While Eric was in a daze watching Lanita, Aaron starts fronting.

"Man, you bugging. You know you ain't gonna talk to her, so let's go skate." While on the floor skating the two were joined by Travis and Jamaal. Travis points out the fact that the girls are on the floor skating as well and trying to push Eric to talk to Lanita.

Cause I'm definitely gonna talk to Jalisa tonight. That's gonna be my girlfriend." Travis says as he has his eyes locked on Jalisa as she skates by. For the rest of the night Travis made good of his word on talking to Jalisa while Eric remained invisible to Lanita.

As time was nearing for the skating rink to close Eric finally built up the nerve to talk to Lanita. The DJ was playing slow songs for couples to dance on or skate on. This song came on called 'Love Changes' by Kashif and Meli'sa Morgan. 'This is it. It's all or nothing.' Eric thought to himself. He skated right next to Lanita, nervous as hell, and asked her to couple skate with him. She took him by the hand and it was if Eric had won a million bucks. He was floating on cloud nine out on the floor. "I hear ya Eeeeee!" Travis said as he skated past holding hands with Jalisa.

Jamaal skated with Marissa while Aaron sat to the side, watching the guys do their thing.

A couple of years later, Eric's schoolboy crush on, now senior, Lanita had toned down a bit but never fully went away. Eric was well into his sophomore year of high school and began to draw interest in his new love, football. In the final game of the season his home town, Altonville, took on cross-town rival, Bateson. Bateson was the favorite and leading 10-6, deep in the fourth quarter. The defensive lineman that started in front of Eric got injured. Bateson needed one more first down to secure a victory and to make it seven years straight over Altonville. Eric's coach called him over. "Eric, I want you to clog that hole up son. Don't you let anybody through" Eric got down in his stance as the quarterback of Bateson counted off. Almost simultaneously with a snap of the ball Eric quickly got out of his stance and shot through the offensive line. He knocked the ball out of the quarterback's hand. Jamaal whom was a starter at the corner position picked the ball up and ran seventy yards to the end zone as the play clock expired. Jamaal's touchdown caught the eye of a certain cheerleader named Marissa. It was a joyous night as Eric was sold on this game of football. His passion for this game would last for years to come.

In the spring, Eric's sister Teresa, whom was also a senior, hosted a birthday party at their parent's house from the garage. Lots of kids were in attendance, it was a big turnout, not to mention she hired a local DJ. As usual Eric was cooling with the guys checking out the girls when suddenly Travis bumped Eric's arm to get his attention. Eric looked over and saw that Lanita, Jalisa, and Marissa had made it to the party.

"Man, you better go rap to her. You know she bout to graduate and all. Last chance, besides, I heard she just broke up with Demetrius." Travis tells Eric.

"And what if she turns me down cold like Jalisa keeps doing you?" Eric asks as Travis pauses for a moment for a quick comeback.

"Oh, I'm starting to wear her down." They laugh as Travis continues. "She can't say no or yes if you don't ever ask." And with that in mind Eric decided that he was going to try his luck with Lanita.

With the guys in puberty, their hormones were in full gear. So when the DJ slowed the music down a bit each one of the guys found a girl to dance with. With a pep talk from Travis earlier and Patti Labelle's 'If only you knew' playing, Eric took a deep breath and walked right over to Lanita. He asked her for a dance and she accepted. While dancing with Lanita, he faced Travis whom was dancing with Jalisa. Travis gave him the thumbs up and was motioning his lips saying talk to her. Jalisa looked at Travis to see what he was doing; Travis then pulled Jalisa closely resting his head next to hers and winked his eye as Eric smiled. Eric then sparked up a conversation, asking Lanita about her plans after high school. They talked for a minute, and then he came on with it.

"Lanita, I know that you're my sister's friend and all, but I like you a lot. A lot... I was wondering if I could be your man."

Eric you're sweet, but I'm too old for you." And just like that Eric's confidence had been shot down. All that he'd feared had come to pass. It was the ultimate, epic fail. Though all was not lost, because just as the song was about to end, the lights were already low when Lanita did the unexpected.

"I do think you're cute though." She said as she looked at him. Right there in the dark she pressed her soft lips against his. Fireworks went off in Eric's head. Though he didn't get the girl, she did give him something sentimental…his first kiss.

Time went on for Eric as he started dating girls while doing his thing in football. When he became a senior, he met his high school sweetheart. After graduation he joined the Marine Corps, married his high school sweetheart, and became a father to twin boys (Devin and Ladarius). A few years later Eric lost his wife in a car accident when the boys were only seven. Eric returned home and began a career in teaching and coaching at his alma mater while continuing to serve in the military until he retired. He persevered at being a good father and put his boys through school. On Friday nights in the fall, he paced the sidelines serving as defensive coordinator/ assistant head coach for his Altonville Titans.

Now at the age of thirty-nine, his twin sons are highly recruited football players approaching their final year of high school. Its early June, Eric sits at a local restaurant called the Eight Sisters Café. He drinks his coffee and reminisce last year's playoffs loss. It was also Eric's final season as assistant coach.

"Excuse me sir, I hear there's a new head coach in town. Is that true?" Eric turns around and sees none other than Travis coming in joking along with Jamaal as they join him for their weekly Saturday morning ritual of coffee at the Eight Sisters' Café. The guys sit down and order their cups of coffee and talk.

"So are you ready to take on this head coaching thing?" Jamaal asks Eric.

"Oh, ain't no doubt." Eric says without a second thought.

"Do you think you're gonna be able to focus with your girl around?" Travis asks. Jamaal cracks a smile as Eric sits there with a distant look on what they're insinuating.

He hadn't heard." Travis tells Jamaal.

"What are y'all talking about?" Eric asks. Travis then lays the local newspaper on the table. Eric takes a look at it. The headline shows the high school's new staff. It includes a picture of Eric being named the new head coach, two new teachers and new assistant principal, Lanita Fields.

"Man that was a long time ago. That's all ancient history now." Eric says to the guys.

Okay ancient history. Don't let me catch you playing archeologist, digging up old bones." Travis says as he and Jamaal laugh. The guys then talk and share some more laughs over coffee.

The following week Eric began his tenure as the new head coach as the team began summer camp. Eric had high expectations for his team as he constantly ranted at his players through long hot days at practice in the summer heat. Through all his gum smacking and loud talking, Eric had a way of bringing out the best in his players.

During the summer, Eric attended a faculty workshop to meet and greet all new staff members. Just before the meeting was in progress, in came Lanita Fields. After a bad relationship with her daughter's father, Lanita put herself through college and is now a proud independent woman. She is petite in stature and just as beautiful as Eric remembered. At the faculty workshop, each person introduced themselves. Afterwards they all socialized as Eric and Lanita finally crossed paths and got a chance to talk. She explained to Eric that she was looking for a house.

"I don't want anything too big. My daughter is in college now, so it's just me." Lanita says.

"Well, there is this place across the street from me for sale. You know it's nice and quiet out there in the boondocks." Eric says to her.

"Hmm, I'll have to look into that, thanks. So how does our football team look this year?"

"The lost in the second round of the playoffs left a bad taste in our mouth. We're ready to get back on the field." Eric says with a bit of fire in his eyes. After a little more catching up and the conclusion of the meeting, the two of them part ways. As Eric said goodbye to Lanita he met another new staff member.

Hi, Iesha Sanders, I'm the new English teacher."

"Eric Daniels, physical ed." he says as they talk momentarily. Iesha was a strikingly beautiful very young lady with a nice figure. She flaunted her curves in a short skirt and a blouse that showed off cleavage from her huge bosom. Eric was fresh off feeling a natural high from his conversation with Lanita that he barely noticed Iesha showing interest as she talked to him. After a talking with Iesha, Eric met a few other members before leaving.

On a Friday morning Eric and his sons were gearing up his boat to go fishing. As they were packing, they noticed a moving truck backing in across the street. Out of the vehicle that followed were Lanita Fields and her sister Jalisa. Eric stood in admiration as Lanita got out of the car wearing this thigh-length sundress, showing off her nice legs. He immediately went across to welcome her to the neighborhood. They talked for minute then Lanita walked inside to assist the movers. Eric watched her walk away and did not notice Jalisa watching him as she unloaded the car.

"After all these years you're still drooling over my big sister. Wow" Jalisa smiles.

"Oh hey girl, how're you doing?" Eric says with excitement as they embrace each other.

"I'm fine mister football coach. How about you?"

"I'm good Miss Doctor of education." Eric says as they talk. Just before Eric leaves, Jalisa invites him to attend Lanita's surprise birthday party in a week. "It's just a small get together, you know, family and friends. Oh, and um tell Travis he's more than welcome to come by as well." she says with a smirk.

After another strenuous week of football practice, it was now Friday. Later that evening, Eric and Travis loaded up an ice chest with beverages. They then went across the street and joined Jamaal and his long time wife Marissa as she and Jalisa were preparing party foods. A few members of Lanita's family came over to her house. As they were all settled, Lanita came pulling up in the driveway being chauffeured by her daughter (Sasha). Lanita got out of the car with the biggest smile, very surprised to see everyone.

During the party Eric, Travis and Jamaal sat among each other and socialized. As most of the guest started to dissipate, the guys were joined by Marissa, Jalisa and Lanita. They began to talk about the old days and growing up in Altonville. Travis started to flirt with Jalisa as usual. Jamaal began to tease Travis about his old crush on Jalisa as they all laugh. Then they both started on Eric. Eric gave off an embarrassing smile as Travis and Jamaal talked about an old rap song he'd wrote about Lanita.

"How did it go?" Travis asked.

"Lanita let me hold your hand and be your man/ and walk you through a land where the sun meets the sand." Jamaal says as he belts out this loud laugh along with Travis and the girls. Eric looks at Lanita as she smiles at him. He then takes a gulp of his beer. "Man y'all go to hell." Eric says as they all laugh.

A few drinks later, Travis and Jalisa are noticeably close. They tell the guys that they are about go to the store and come right back. "I don't think their coming back." Marissa says of Travis and Jalisa as they pull out of the driveway. Moments later, after a brief clean up, Marissa, Jamaal, and Eric say goodnight.

The next morning, Eric and Jamaal were having their Saturday morning coffee at the Eight Sister's Café. Travis finally came in to join them.

"Well, look what the cat drug in." Jamaal says.

"Looks like somebody had a long night. I thought you guys were coming right back." Eric says to Travis.

"We got stuck in traffic." Travis says with a smirk. The guys then laugh and carry on with their coffee and conversation.

Later on Eric and his sons were installing revamped leather seats into this old 1966 Pontiac GTO. Eric purchased it to restore in his spare time as a hobby and to bond with his sons. While working on the car, Eric talks with his sons on some of life's little lessons. As usual they listen, then in a moment's notice they began to joke around and heckle Eric. While Eric and his sons were talking, Lanita and Sasha walk over to return Eric's ice chest from the night before. Everyone was mutually introduced.

The boys invite Sasha to the bowling alley as Eric and Lanita talk. He walked her back across the street on to her front porch. They sat in the swing that hung from the ceiling of her porch as they did some catching up. They discussed being single parents after he told her about losing his wife when the boys were little.

"I'd never really introduce my lady friends to my boys. Not saying I get around cause I don't, I just don't want them to see me as a womanizer and think that it's okay. Enough about me, I see the apple didn't fall too far from the tree. She seems to be a lot like you." Eric says of her daughter.

"Yeah she's my little mini me. You've done a nice job as well, your boys look like a couple of nice young men."

"They're some good boys when they listen. I like teaching them to fix or build stuff."

That's nice. Speaking of building things, do you know anyone around here that builds patios? I want one on the back." Lanita says. Eric told her that he knew a few people that could do it. "-or if you want to save a lot of money, I could do it." He says.

Days later Eric drew up plans, picked up supplies, and began building the patio. He worked on it during the week after football practice. Lanita admired his work ethic and helped out when his sons weren't around as they began to develop a close friendship.

On Saturday morning, after meeting with the guys, Eric went to Lanita's house.

"Good morning neighbor, I was about to get started and I didn't want to startle you. I also bought you some coffee." He says as he hands her the cup.

"Thanks Eric, if you need anything come in and let me know. I'll be out soon as I can wake up. I was up late on the phone with Jalisa last night." She says.

Eric walks around the house and began working. Lanita drinks her coffee and watches television. She then finds something to wear and takes a morning shower. After showering she realizes she needs a towel from the utility room. While Eric was working, he ran out of nails. He came in to see if Lanita needed anything while he was out. "Hey, I'm gonna... Whoa..." He paused seeing her standing there drenched in her birthday suit as the water beaded down her beautiful brown skin. She gasps as he turned his head and she quickly grabbed a towel to cover herself. "I'm on my way to the store. Just wanted to know if you needed anythighs, I mean any**thing**... if you need any**thing**." Eric sighed as he could only walk away.

That Monday marked the first day of the new school year. Eric ran into Lanita as she was coming into the school with a box of office supplies. She looked very appealing, Eric thought to himself, with her new hairdo, eyeglasses and skirt suit. "Let me get that for you." He quickly got the box and toted it to her office for her. Both with the little mishap from the other day still in mind as Lanita breaks the ice. "I didn't quite have my office ready. I guess it's not the first time I got caught with my pants down huh" she says as they laugh and joke about what happened the other day. She expresses how embarrassed she felt. "Trust me; you don't have anything to be embarrassed about." Eric says in a flirting manner as Lanita smiles and takes his comment into consideration.

Eric then walks the hall greeting the children and some of his football players. He runs into Iesha on the hall whom is headed to her classroom. She seemed enthused to see him. She compliments Eric on how his polo shirt fits him well, showing off his physical features. Iesha pointed out her classroom and told Eric that he was more than welcome to stop by anytime during the day.

On Friday night, Eric had his inaugural game as the new head coach. He paced the sideline, talking loudly to his players and smacking on gum. Eric occasionally threw his hat to the ground as he argued calls by the referees. After all was said and done, Altonville won the game 34-3. Eric and his team shook hands with the opposing team. As he headed to the locker room, Lanita stood by the fence. "Hey coach, good game. We'll work on that intensity some other time." She smiles as he walks to the locker room.

Weeks went by as the Altonville Titans kept on winning. Eric and Lanita's friendship was blossoming as he was becoming her very own personal handyman. He fixed her sink, stove and occasionally did maintenance on her car. In her own way she began to see Eric for the man he'd become and not just the little brother of one of her old friends.

On a cloudy Saturday evening Eric was working on his car while the boys were at his parent's house. Lanita walks across the street into the garage where he is and strikes up a conversation. As he works on his car wearing his well fitted tank top Lanita takes notice of his USMC tattoo on his left bulging bicep. Eric gets a couple of beers out of his antique ice box and gives her one. "You spend so much time on this old car. Does it even run?" she asked. "I'll tell you what, give about thirty minutes to wash up and I'll take you for a spin in it."

Eric invited her in while he freshened up and took Lanita for a ride as he promised. They rode through the blocks of Altonville and passed closed buildings and empty lots where some of their old hangouts once stood. He even took her to the park where they walked around as the street lights lit the way. They sat next to each other in the swings on the playground and reminisced for a while. After the lightning started to flicker, they started walking back to the car as the wind began blowing.

I remember this used to be the place to be every Sunday in the summer. There was basketball, softball, swimming, or people just riding through showing off their rides. This place was so full of life." Lanita recalls.

"I remember the first time I saw you. You were standing right over talking to Teresa. I remember thinking to myself how beautiful you were. I must've thought about you all night long." he reminisces as Lanita smiles at him. "I was too shy to talk to you back then, but you were always my girl." he says as he looks at her.

"Oh really"

"Yeah, and you still are" Eric says as he takes Lanita by the hand while walking to the car.

It was the first time Eric ever told Lanita how he felt about her without stuttering or stumbling over words. As for Lanita, it was the first time in a long time she allowed herself to feel this way about any one. Eric walked her to the passenger door. Instead of opening the door Eric gently places his hands on Lanita's hips. He then turned her around and started kissing her deeply. As they kissed they paid little attention to the inclement weather that was blowing in. They ignored the wind getting stronger and the rumbles of thunder in the background. Once the cold droplets of rain started to fall they could ignore it no longer as they got in the car. Lanita slid right next to Eric in the car as he took her home.

They arrived at her place and raced inside out of the rain. Eric was about to leave. "You're not going to go back out in that are you?" Lanita asks. "Well, yeah" he simply responds. "Are you sure you want too?" Lanita asks in a soft voice as she gives Eric an inviting look. Eric walks to her and starts kissing her again and holding her tightly. Lanita began to breathe heavily. She caressed Eric's head and whispered his name as he kissed her on the neck. Eric lifted Lanita up and toted her to the bedroom.

As they undressed, their clothing fell to the floor like autumn leaves. Eric kissed her on the back of the shoulder while undoing her bra and shedding her panty's. He held her at the waist as the moisture of her womanhood invited his swollen shaft in. Lanita lustfully groans while biting her lower lip and grasping the bed sheets with both hands. Eric continuously penetrates her, grinding her harder and harder with his overwhelmed desire for her. "Oh Yes Eric!" Lanita says passionately as she grimaces looking back at him. He clutches her waist tighter and strokes her faster. Lanita cries out as Eric explodes inside of her. He grunts and exhales as she turns around in his arms. Lanita rested her head on Eric's chest and lied in his arms on her bed during the storm. Lanita Fields, the girl in which he'd admired for a long time was now lying here in his arms.

Once the rain went away Eric got dressed. Lanita put on a silk housecoat and walked Eric to the door. He held her in his arms and was about to say goodnight. She felt him stiffen up once more while pressed against him. "Looks like someone's not ready to go" She says as she looks at him with her back to the door. Eric took one look of her body inside of that undone housecoat and could not resist the need to get back inside of her. Right there at the door, he unbuckles his pants. He lifts her off of the floor as she wraps her legs around his waist. Eric eases her down on his stiffened shaft. In an erotically charged rhythm they began to move. She swirled her hips while staring deeply into his eyes as he flopped around inside of her. "Right there, Right there" Lanita says as she holds him tight. Eric got more intense and grinded harder as Lanita interlocked her legs tightly with his as he climaxed with her. Eric and Lanita finally say goodnight. Eric drags himself into his car and backs across the street.

The following week was homecoming. On Friday the school's alumni toured the school. Eric stopped by Lanita's office to talk. Though they decided to keep their relationship under wraps until the time was right, Eric flirted with Lanita every chance he got. "Eric you are so bad." Lanita says as Eric was trying to steal a kiss in her office. They were interrupted by his best friend Aaron Henry, his girlfriend Tatiana Perez and her daughter Jasmine. Aaron was in town for his class reunion. Aaron introduced Tatiana to Eric and Lanita. They talked for a little while before enjoying the rest of the tour and the big pep rally.

That night Altonville dismantled cross-town rival Bateson 38-0. No one was happier than Eric about that win. He attended the homecoming dance where he ran into Lanita whom was an assistant chaperone at the dance. He somehow convinced her to go celebrate with him. As a result they went to crash Aaron's class reunion. Eric and Lanita went in and mingled with the crowd. Before she knew it Eric was by the DJ with the microphone. "The roof, the roof, the roof is on fire!" Eric becomes the life of the party as Lanita laughs. It was the most fun Lanita's had with anyone in a while.

One night as Lanita was preparing for bed she was having another long conversation with Jalisa. During their talk, Lanita mentioned Eric's name more times than she'd realized.

"Are you and Eric messing around?"

"No, why do say that?"

"Well, you keep on saying Eric this and Eric that. What's really going on Stella?" Jalisa says. Even though Jalisa's only teasing with her sister, Lanita realizes that maybe she is getting in over her head about Eric. Though she's dated other guys, none of them made her feel the way Eric has. Every night ended with a text from Eric that simply read 'Goodnight Beautiful XOXO'.

They say that Hell hath no fury like a woman scorned. After a long stressful relationship with her daughter's father, Lanita became this proud and independent woman for a long time. She refused to let her guard down for any man. Just the thought of her falling for Eric, to her, seemed ludicrous. Due to what happened the last time she gave her heart away, it now scared her to feel this way. She felt like the only way to stop her growing desire for Eric was to stop seeing him all together. Lanita tried desperately to find the correct way and the appropriate time to handle this situation. During the week they both were so busy and caught up in work.

Lanita walked over to Eric's place on a cold fall Saturday evening. She had every intention of ending this fling with him. She knocks at the door a couple of times. He then comes to the door and invites her in. Lanita comes in and smells this mouthwatering aroma of rosemary chicken coming from the kitchen.

You must've been reading my mind. I was just about to call you." Eric says.

Eric we need to talk."

"-I already know what you're going to say."

"You do"

"Yes, I've been so busy trying to prepare the team for the play-offs that I haven't had time to spend with you. So I wanted to make it up to you tonight." Eric says as he sits her at his candle-lit dining room table. He then brought her dinner to the table along with a glass of wine. It was the perfect setting. Just seeing Eric so enthused and putting forth the effort into making a romantic evening with her, Lanita chose not to tell him of her intentions. With the boys hanging out with their cousin's for the night, Eric and Lanita enjoyed a nice quiet diner.

After dinner they sat in front of the fireplace and continued to talk and take down more wine. The more they talked, the more Lanita was feeling Eric, though she was trying desperately not to show it. Things started to get a little heavy when Eric told Lanita how he's always felt about her. "I've wanted to have moments like this with you for a long time." He says as brushed her forearm gently with one of the roses. He then leaned closer and kissed her softly. The feel of his soft lips pressed against hers sent arousing shockwaves throughout her body. Lanita continued to fight her feelings towards Eric as she stood up in front of the fireplace on an attempt to leave.

Eric stood up and held her in his arms trying to convince her to stay. There on the verge of her vulnerability she could no longer fight it as they engaged in a deep kiss. With lustful moans they began to shed each other's garments onto the carpet. Eric got on top of Lanita in front of the fireplace. She held him tight as their tongues teased in a tantalizing tango. Eric kissed Lanita down as he undid her bra and circled his tongue around her stiffened nipples. He then removed her pink laced panties and kissed her body down to the depts as she rolled her eyes back and bit down on her lower lip. Lanita arched her back as she breathed heavily. Eric got back on top of Lanita easing his way inside of her slowly as they looked deep into each other's eyes. With her toes in a curled position, Lanita held him tight as he grinded her harder and faster until they reached the pinnacle of pleasure. Eric collapsed on Lanita's chest to catch his breath as she held him in her arms and caressed his head. Later they cuddled on the sofa in front of the television until about three o' clock in the morning.

The following week Eric and Lanita were back to their busy schedule at work. After school and football practice Eric studied game film with his assistant coaches. One evening as Eric was in his office with the other coaches when he got a surprise visit from Lanita. They stepped outside to talk in private. They talked as she told him that she wanted end their relationship.

"What's going on? I thought we had something good here." Eric says to her.

"It's not you, it's me. I just need to sort some things out." she tells him.

"Yeah, I've heard that before. It's usually followed by some other dude." A disappointed Eric says.

"Come on Eric, after all you've done for me I wouldn't do that to you. I just need some time that's all. Please don't be upset with me. I still would love very much to be your friend." Lanita says as she takes him by the hand. She gave him a hug then on this cold late fall evening Eric watched the love of his life walk away.

After a close win in the team's first playoff game on Friday night, Eric joined Travis and Jamaal for coffee at the Eight Sisters Café the next morning. The guys sat at their table and talked about the game. As they discussed the game Iesha came into the café for breakfast. She spoke to the guys. "That was some game last night. You guys had me on pins and needles, but I knew if anybody could pull it off, you could coach." Iesha says as she smiles at him then goes on to place her order. The guys took notice on how Iesha was so into Eric. They look at each other then give Eric the look.

"Well damn, who is that?" Travis says as he was checking her out.

"Yeah Coach... Who is that?" Jamaal says.

"If that's one of the cheerleaders, you have some explaining to do." Travis jokes with Eric who in turn shakes his head. Eric then explains that Iesha is just a coworker of his. The guy's conversation then changes as they begin to pester Eric about Lanita. "Lanita and I are just friends. That's all we ever were and that's all we'll ever be." Eric says trying to convince Travis and Jamaal that he no longer has a thing for Lanita. The three of them then continue to enjoy their Saturday morning coffee.

One day on the following week Lanita made a few rounds throughout the school campus. As she came to the office she saw Devin and Ladarius waiting to see the principal. She then took them into her office. "What are you boys doing up here." she asked. She then found out that they were horse playing in class.

"You boys are young men now. You should be preparing for college. You can't be doing silly things such as this. What's your father going to think?" Lanita says to the boys as she sits behind her desk.

"You're right Ms. Fields. He already has enough on his mind right now with the playoffs and all...and this thing he has for you." Devin says with a grin as Ladarius bumps him on the arm and smiles as well.

"Wait what, who told you boys that?"

"Come on Ms. Fields we're not babies." Devin says.

"Yeah, we see how he looks at you." Ladarius adds as Devin and he joke with her. Lanita was embarrassed as she tried desperately to hold a straight face. She sent the boys out of her office and back to class.

That evening Eric had just got his car back from the paint shop. Though it was almost dark, Eric was still admiring the fresh black paint job on his car. He stands with pride thinking of all the work that was put into the car from the engine to the interior and now the body. His car was now fully restored as he stood in awe. As he was outside he looked across and saw Lanita getting out of her car with her gym bag. Eric wanted badly to call her over and talk, but he just held his composure as she went inside.

The next day Iesha was standing in the hall in front of the principal's office talking with Lanita about some things to improve her class. As they talked Lanita held an envelope, hoping to catch Eric as he routinely passed the office at this point of the day. He came by as she gave him the envelope. "Coach Daniels, this was addressed to you." she says as she took notice to the small talk and lack of eye contact. Iesha then spoke to Eric flashing her beautiful smile and dimples. Eric spoke to her as well. He then walked back down the hall. "He is so fine." Iesha says while checking out Eric. Lanita looks at her wanting to say something instead she just kept it to herself.

That Saturday Eric and his sons were attending a college football game of one the schools that was recruiting the boys. That night Lanita was having girl's night out with Jalisa and Marissa. After dining out and a movie, the girls enjoyed a bottle of wine at Lanita's as they talked. While they were talking Jalisa's phone went off.

"Somebody's getting a booty call." Marissa says to Lanita as they smile.

"Oh that's just Travis texting. I told him I was in town." Jalisa says. Lanita and Marissa then look at each. "booty call" They say together and laugh.

"Whatever... Jamaal just better hope you don't have too many of these." Jalisa tells Marissa as she holds her glass up. Jalisa then begins teasing Lanita about Eric.

"Why you are so persistent that he and I have this thing? Eric is sweet, but I'm not sure he wants to be with someone like me. I'm not the easiest person to get along with at times." Lanita says.

"Girl, you're that way because you chose to be. Don't make him pay for what William did to you." Jalisa says to her as Marissa agrees. "Besides we know you got a soft spot for E." Jalisa jokes.

"Speaking of Eric, I hear they're offering a huge salary to coach at Miles High School next year." Marissa says to Lanita who was clueless about this. Lanita then thought back to the letter she gave Eric the other day at school.

Later on after Marissa and Jalisa left, Lanita treated herself to a long hot bubble bath. She soaked in relaxation of her steamy bath as she listened to complete silence. Lanita thought about the things Jalisa said to her earlier. She began to think about those special moments she shared with Eric. Though Lanita put on this independent image, she could not deny how complete she felt when she was with Eric.

The following Monday, Eric put an end to the rumors of him leaving to coach elsewhere as he and Lanita finally talked. During

his break, Lanita came to his office. She knocked at the door and came in. Eric was sitting at his computer with Iesha standing behind him with her hands on his shoulders in a massaging position as they share a laugh. "Hey I hope I'm not interrupting anything. Coach Daniels, I need to have a word with you… alone." Lanita says. "I'll see you later Coach." Iesha says sweeping her hand across his back. Lanita watched Iesha leave the room then looked at Eric feeling every bit of the lioness zodiac sign that represents her. Eric explains that Iesha was helping him load a program on his computer.

"Yeah from the look of it she's trying to help herself to something else." Lanita says with an attitude.

"Wait, you think that Ms. Sanders and I… Come on Nita, this girl is way too young for me. It's not like that, even if that was the case it wouldn't last."

"Why do you say that?" Lanita asks as she sits next to Eric at his desk. He points out his playbook.

"See all these X's and O's? I know this game backwards, forwards and upside down. But when it comes to the game of X's and O's that deals with the heart, I lose every time." Eric says depressingly.

"You know, being without you these few weeks have been crazy. I know how you feel about me, in fact I've always known. What I didn't know is that I was going to fall in love with you. I do want to be with you Eric. You're an amazing man, but it's so hard for me to love anyone after going through what I went through with Sasha's father. He was so controlling and mentally abusive." Lanita emotionally explains as Eric swivels his chair facing her. He then places her hands in his.

"I'm not him, I know your worth. I always have." Eric says as Lanita gets teary eyed behind her glasses.

"You always know just what to say to me Eric." Lanita says as she sniffles.

"I'm just being honest. Lanita, it's evident that we want to be together. **Are** we going to be together? I'm not saying let's get married right off. Let's see where this leads." he says as she nods her head. She then gives him a big hug before leaving his office as he gets started with his next class.

On Friday night the Altonville Titans faced off in a revenge game against the team that knocked them out of the playoffs the previous year. This time it was for the championship. It was a tough battle. Altonville walked away victorious with a 15-7 win. For the first time since the early 80's the Titans were the toast of the town. After the championship Eric spent a week of doing interviews for local news stations and newspapers. During their championship pep rally, Iesha came over to Lanita to apologize. "I had no idea that you two were, ya know." Iesha says. "Oh girl it's alright." Lanita tells her as they talk

One evening after leaving his office, Eric walked out into the stands of the stadium reminiscing his team's great season. He was soon joined by Lanita.

"Eric, I've been looking all over for you. What are you doing out here in the cold?"

"I'm just reveling."

"Couldn't you find a warmer place to revel?" she says wearing this big jacket with her arms folded.

"It's not so bad. Once you're in it for a little while, you kind of get use to it." Eric subliminally says to a quick witted Lanita.

"Well, maybe it's time we both come in from it." she says as they engage in the biggest kiss. They then left the stadium together.

Eric and Lanita embarked upon a beautiful and devoted relationship. He was everything she ever wanted as she was for him.